MW00966259

The Outsider's Mind

A Collection of Short Stories and the Quotes They Inspired
By Sean Aeon

THE OUTSIDER'S MIND

*A Collection of Short Stories
and the Quotes They Inspired*

SEAN AEON

www.seanaeon.com
ISBN 978-1-7351519-1-5
LCCN 2020910073
First Edition
Editor: Amy Cleveland
Cover Art: Samantha Lundy

This book is dedicated to my extraordinary mother, who unfortunately didn't get to see what all of her sacrifice and time invested in me amounted to.

And, also to everyone that I've met along the way who selflessly helped me, believed in me, and encouraged me to continue moving forward creatively: Riley, Debby, Lashawn, Jatia, Renaya, Chris, Doreen, Kendall, Jay, Khiah, Erika, Salma, Octavia, Julius, Laquita, Paloma, Marc, Amy, Jess, Jen, Sam, Nicole, and Logan.

INTRODUCTION

The Outsider's Mind is a collection of stories about outcasts, a position we all occupy at one time or another. In each story a glimpse into the perspective of another outsider is revealed—how they see the world, how they believe the world sees them, as well as how they see themselves. What intrigues me the most are the thoughts that precede and follow one's actions, along with the narratives we tell ourselves that reside in the spaces between the words we hear and speak. It's these silent and nuanced aspects that we'll be exploring in unlikely ways, through stories and characters that range from the strange to the spectacular.

I've chosen to open this book with quotes from each story along with the philosophies that will be presented. My hope is that these snapshots will add another layer to the reading experience, firstly by being a guide. Not sure what you feel like reading? You can browse through the quotes until an idea speaks to you, and then dive into the full story to see how that one piece is a part of a larger mosaic. Or, maybe today is just a quotes kind of day, and reading a few thought-provoking sentences is all you need to ignite a spark in your mind.

The art I personally enjoy the most is usually not only pleasing to the senses, but also provides a degree of insightfulness. Why that's special is because it allows our entertainment to also be enriching. We give someone's creation our attention, and we get rewarded with something in return we can take with us. If there's a goal in mind with this book—and why I truly believe it's worth reading—it would be to stimulate thoughts and conversations that aren't necessarily always at the forefront, to view life in a deeper and more meaningful manner, and to consider why we view life the way that we do. I see *that* as the beauty of philosophy: to open the doors within us we didn't know were locked.

I hope you enjoy what you find inside the outsider's mind.

INSIGHT: SELF

I dispatched my demons
without first
understanding them,
so I was bound to become
a demon myself.

— Augmented: Submersion

One can be so good
at seeing what's
out of place,
that soon even
that which is in its
proper position can
spark skepticism.

– Uneven

If it takes someone
being *like* me
for them to like me,
I hope we never have
anything in common.

— The Undead Eye: Kennedy

From the monster
we feed,
grows a monster that
feeds upon us.

- Augmented: Source

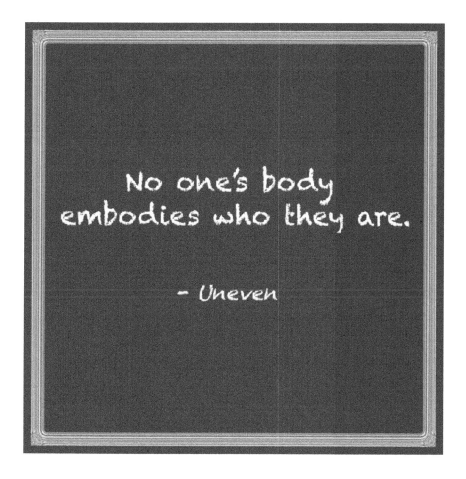

No one's body
embodies who they are.

- Uneven

We hope to never be
in a situation where we
require the same assistance
that we offer to others,
but in many ways,
that's the only way to
understand what it is
that we offer at all.

- The Undead Eye: Dr. Gren

Time taught me that
time doesn't change us,
it unfolds us,
like the recipient of
a handwritten letter.
Each section that's turned
to face the reader only
reveals more and more
of what lay inside all along.

— *Augmented: Submersion*

The easiest lie
for people to tell
is the one that
hides something
they're ashamed of.

- The Undead Eye: Dr. Gren

The drawback to one
numbing their pain
is that eventually
a line is crossed,
and they can no
longer feel when
they're making it worse.

– Uneven 3

People think they
know you
because they knew you,
even if the person
you were isn't the
person you are;
even if the person you
used to be is dead.

— The Undead Eye: Will

There are few things more fatal to who one is than being misunderstood, and few things more fatal to a collective than misinformation.

- Another Way: Jerome

What we believe
will always be
more powerful
than what's real.

- The Undead Eye: Dr. Gren

The easiest thing for
people to forget
is what you've
done for them.

– Uneven 3

Playtime for adults
is about running as
far away from
the person they've become,
in order to find—
even for a moment—
the person they truly are.

– For Hire: Apprentice

Maybe I was also
unable to properly assess
the true value of
what I had,
because I was
constantly comparing it
to something else.

— The Undead Eye: Will

A calm environment
can feel like an
aggressive one if,
I myself, am aggressive.

- Augmented: Submersion

Never expect anything
from anyone,
especially not the truth.
As long as you remember
that anything anyone
says to you could be a lie,
you'll never be
disappointed.

— Uneven 2

He found that the truth
is often requested,
but what's truly desired is
something that one
already agrees with.

— Uneven

They must need something
to believe in that
makes them feel better,
even if they know
it's not true.
They must want it
even if the only thing
it provides them with
is the illusion of security.

— The Undead Eye: Will

It was never
my plan to settle,
to deify the lesser
of two evils,
worship it as my savior,
and live ensnared in
a religion of
my own creation.

- Augmented: Inquiry

THE PHILOSOPHY

The Catalytic Principle

Neither right nor wrong exist, there are only catalysts and non-catalysts. Either a person, action, or situation causes change, or it does not. Whether the catalysts are viewed as positive or negative is a perspective of one's own invention to more easily compartmentalize the way in which they are affected.

Falsehood Theory

A lie is the truth had circumstances been different. It's a believable alternative to a provable fact or sincere point of view, so all that *really* separates a lie from the truth is a thorough imagination. In essence, lies and truths are in the same category—they're both stories one chooses to accept or deny.

The Base Barter Principle

Between two interacting entities there's always a level of physical or mental exchange; one's goods for another's services. Although it may go undetected by one, or both parties, and that which is exchanged may not be directly proportional, it exists and transpires nevertheless. Even those who give freely expect to trade their generosity for gratitude.

Authorist Futurism

An Authorist acknowledges that the only
thing ahead of them is a blank canvas.
They believe the composition to fill
that canvas is decided by nothing short
of what they want for themselves, their
will and determination to create it,
and their readiness to see that what
they intended may have taken on a
different form, and presented a
progressive opportunity that they could
not have previously foreseen.
Authorist Futurism encapsulates vision,
action, and fluidity.

Surrenderist Futurism

A Surrenderist accepts that their *present* forecasts the unalterable events of their *future*. Consequently, they would surrender to said forecasted outcome, presuming they could no longer affect it through any fathomable action of their own, or foreseeable action from another. Surrenderist Futurism encapsulates hope, inaction, and acceptance.

General Ownership Phenomenon

We are born into a world grounded in
the illusionary ideal of possession—
from the items we purchase, create,
and collect; to the people we
befriend, give birth to, and love; to
the bodies we inhabit and utilize to
experience internal and external stimuli
(the creation and capture of memories),
it's simply a matter of time or
circumstance before all is proven
impermanent. The illusion of ownership
is then revealed to be the most feeble,
and ultimately destructive, device used
by humanity to validate their existence,
because the promise and expectation of
permanence will either be revealed as
deception or failure. The volatility of
our environment may seem like another
bitter, unsightly facet of life, but, it's
actually the reason why life is worth
living; presenting us with a dazzling
opportunity: to be in a state of constant
wonder and gratitude. We own nothing, we
keep nothing, therefore we lose nothing—
we are free. Everything is borrowed.

Stabilizing Assimilation Law

The unconsciously or consciously objective
recognition of a personal disconnect
regarding what's viewed to be acceptable of
ones species—on the most elementary of
philosophical and psychological levels—and
the understanding that for the maintenance
of daily mental stability, one must retain
a level of adherence to that which has been
generally accepted as natural. In other words,
if one is assimilation deficient, they will
always question every action, thought, and
inclination regarding what it means to be
alive, or dead, or human, or non-human.
They'll accept nothing as simply being the way
that it is—not even aspects of themselves—but
they'll see that in order to make it through
each day, it's necessary to view existence as
others do who, for whatever reason, see less
to question, or nothing to question at all.

The Principle of Emotional Truth

Emotional Truth is always changing, as is
characteristic of emotions themselves.
Emotional Truth is that which is true only
in the moment that it's experienced. The
words are felt to be true when they are
said, the actions are felt to be true when
they are performed, and the thoughts are
felt to be true when they are thought of,
but prior to that moment, they didn't
exist and after that moment, they are
lifeless until brought back to life
once more.

Displeasing Decision Consolation

When having to choose between two undesirable options, this is the process of making oneself more at ease with the decision by creating, or manipulating, aspects of the selected choice into a more favorable light—albeit a false one. This allows one to produce a convincing scenario where they have an appreciation of something they never wanted to begin with, therefore decreasing the possibility of increasing dissatisfaction and disappointment regarding their selection. In other words, if one can either invent or imagine a set of desired characteristics about a selection they never wanted, they can fool themselves into liking, or even loving, something they previously never cared for.

THE UNDEAD EYE: WILL

My head really hurts. Bad. Actually, everything hurts all the time, but my head hurts the worst. Then there's my stomach—I can always feel it— it's like stray dogs fighting in the shadows of an alley on trash day. They're growling, biting, and scratching each other over a meat-speckled bone; imagine that happening in the center of your body every time you move. And there's no one that I can tell about it, no one who wants to hear about it anyway, because we're all like this. We all feel the pain inside, so there's nothing about it that's worth sharing. By "all of us" I mean those around me—those *like me*—the ones who are sick. Not everyone is sick, I've seen them. They look the way I used to, but I only remember the way I used to look when I see them, and I hate them for it. I don't want to hate them, I don't want to be filled with rage, but I am. I hate them for reminding me of everything that I've lost just as I've finally been able to forget that I ever had it. A part of me knows it's not their fault, but it doesn't matter. Part of this sickness is that I'm usually not in control, no matter how much I want to be, I'm not. I can't understand things the way that they really are any longer, and the fact that I can't understand and I'm not who I used to be fills me with rage even more. It makes the stray dogs fighting inside of me hungrier, and they fight even more ferociously. They make me want to fight; they give me my strength, frankly, they give me everything that I have left: my purpose, my motivation—everything. I don't have much of anything else anymore. I have the clothes I'm wearing that I try to clean sometimes, but it's hard to do certain things when you're sick. It's hard to do a lot of the things that you need to when you've lost so much of yourself, and it's hard to focus when you're consumed with everything that you've lost. Those people, the ones who aren't sick, they think they have more than I do. They think they have something I don't—they're wrong. Everything is borrowed[1].

My eyes are still closed, but I'm only pretending to be asleep—just like everyone else that's sick—because I don't sleep anymore. I just close my eyes and keep them closed because, from what I can remember, that's what sleep used to be like. That's how it used to work, right? I would lower my eyelids and, like sleight of hand, the next thing I knew I would wake up from sleeping feeling rested and renewed. Now, I just close my eyes, refuse to open them, and wait to hear something that makes me react. That's what everyone does once they're sick, because you don't sleep anymore. Your body doesn't want sleep. There's too much pain, too much

---

[1] *The General Ownership Phenomenon:* We are born into a world grounded in the illusionary ideal of possession. From the items we purchase, create, and collect, to the people we befriend, give birth to, and love, to the bodies we inhabit and utilize to experience internal and external stimuli (the creation and capture of memories), it's only a matter of time or circumstance before all is proven impermanent. The illusion of ownership is then revealed to be the most feeble and ultimately destructive device used by humanity to validate their existence, because the promise and expectation of permanence will either be revealed as deception or failure. The volatility of our environment may seem like another bitter, unsightly facet of life, but in actuality, it's the reason why life is worth living; presenting us with a dazzling opportunity: to be in a state of constant wonder and gratitude. We own nothing, we keep nothing, therefore we lose nothing—we are free. Everything is borrowed.

rage, too much of everything you don't want, but, it's yours now—more than that—it's you. It's like when anger takes control: everything that you don't want becomes everything that defines you. That's what my sickness is. That's the disease. So, I try to keep my eyes closed for as long as I can, because then I don't have to see what the disease has done to me. I'll always feel it, but at least I can pretend that what I'm feeling is something else, something…something's happening. I have to open my eyes now whether I want to or not. Right now. It's still dark in this room inside what used to be someone's home. I like that I've found an empty corner, the corners are the safest. Here I have a measure of privacy and security, almost like before I was sick; like walking hand-in-hand with your parents, one on each side of you, and they're your protection, they're your protection from the rest of the whole world. I like when my back is against the wall, at least I know that everything I need to face is right in front of me. No surprises.

Someone is opening the door to the house—I was right, something *is* happening—and three more sets of eyes slowly open. There is one of us sitting in each corner of the room—the stray dogs are now all too real. "Hello?" A woman's voice, delicate and unassuming. "Are you serious?!" A man's voice quickly follows. He sounds very different from her: hardened, maybe paranoid. He could have a gun on him. I should care about the possibility of a gun, it *should* make a difference to me—scare me—but what do I have to lose? At the entrance of the house there's a small foyer and stairs on the right that go up to the second floor; on the left is the dining room that's slightly sectioned off with a doorless entryway. Once through the threshold, nestled in the shadows, the three others and I are waiting. And my head hurts. The glow from the streetlights outside spill through the blinds, painting soft, parallel rays across the room. I know if I glance down I can see the opening in my torso where the flesh has fallen away, and the bones from my ribs are exposed. As I hear the man and the woman both cautiously approaching, about to turn into the room, fear appears as such a sloppily backward concept: they're scared—terrified—because they think that they have something to lose, and I am fearless because I have lost everything. So, which one of us is truly more sick?

"It's quiet, I really think it's fine here." The woman, whispering loudly, is apparently on my side tonight. "Okay, *yes*, but can you just *please* be quiet, please? We need to check it out first." The man whispers back—from the sound of it, he'd be able to survive much longer without the woman and her whispers.

I've never seen the others who are in the room with me before, I just know that they're sick like me, so I'll have to find my patience. The man and the woman cross the entrance into the room, and are moving to the center where they can be better illuminated—the rage immediately swells within me like yeast baking in an oven: even though only dimly lit, it's clear they're both physically picturesque. The man is tall and in shape, with sharply angled facial features framed by thick, curly hair on his head and face. The woman is of average height with curves that her jacket can't hide, full lips and expressive eyes sitting beneath eye lashes that stand at attention. I'm sure their parents are quite pleased by their pairing—if they're alive. From what I can see, they both have something on their backs—sleeping bags or supplies maybe— but there's also something else. The other three in the room with me don't wait to find out, they rise up groaning loudly and spring their attack. I sound the same way too, with the groaning. When you get sick, something about the disease gets to that part of your brain first: your speech. Initially it's subtle, you sound like maybe you've just had too much to drink—slurring a few of your words—but then one day you wake up, and the things you were able to say that used to matter so much are replaced with abrasive, gargled groans, and then it's not so subtle anymore. I don't miss it though— the talking—the words weren't even important, only the actions that the words implied. The words themselves only got in the way. Words make you believe things that aren't real yet, and maybe never will be. Now, I know to wait and watch, because the words are worthless.

Not even *I* know what the three others are saying or trying to say—if anything—but they're all up, and they're groaning, and I was right to let them go first. "Quick, Riley, now!" No more whispers. The unassuming woman racks a shotgun— *BANG!* I was almost right, but it seems that the paranoid man is also too shaky to handle firearms. The blast rips apart the top half of their nearest pursuer, and what's left of the body tips and falls to one side like it was just chopped down by a lumberjack. I'm in one of the corners nearest to the entrance of the room—just slightly behind, and to the left of the man and woman at this point—desperately holding myself back. Every part of my body wants to feast! It's like my elbows, ankles, fingers—everything, everything needs to be fed. I *am* hunger. The shotgun racks again—*BANG!* One more to go and then it's my tur— "Too loud daddy." A new voice protests. A chihuahua-sized, muffled voice came from where the man's standing—there's someone else with them. "I'm sorry, pretty girl, it's almost done though, okay?" Is the man talking to a child? He must have a child tucked under his jacket. The shotgun racks—*BANG!* Again—*BANG!* The woman is panting heavily. "That was the last of—" I interrupt her pointless explanation. Locking my hands around both the man and the woman's lower-legs, I let the devastating strength of the ravenous animals inside of me guide my movements. With one yank both of them fly to the ground. The woman's gun escapes her grip and lands a few feet away —stuck in what's left of one of the freshly inanimate corpses. While they're momentarily disoriented, I move as fast as I can to deal with the shooter first. I crawl on top of her and move my head back as far as it can go, swing it down towards her's —the impact is mildly jarring—then pull my head back hard and fast, and let an ocean's worth of pressure rush away from my face. There's been a rod of some kind stuck in my skull, for I think a few days now, but now it's stuck in the woman's skull and she can't even feel it—that's much better. My head has a leak now, but I can do something about that after I eat. I pull the rod out of the woman's head, and smash it back down again—finally. There's a nice big opening now where the bone shattered. I put the rod down, claw the brains out with my hands, and shovel them into my mouth. There's blood everywhere, which is why my clothes are always dirty. I needed to eat, I needed this—it's *so* good. It's odd how many people just blindly wander into places they're completely unfamiliar with, places where they can't confirm whether or not it's safe. Maybe they're so scared of where they've been that anywhere else seems like a safe haven—I wonder if I was like that? Maybe I was also unable to properly assess the true value of what I had, because I was constantly comparing it to something else—who knows. That's not something that concerns me now.

It's hard for me to keep track of time since I've been sick. Whatever mind I have left appears to only be enough for the present moment, a few of the moments that led me here, and a bit of general contemplation. This woman's my food now, and I bet she spent the whole day worrying about how not to be food. Did she appreciate anything good that happened today unless it had to do with her not being food? And now look, she still ended up being food. Did she waste her last day alive filled with anxiety, and stripped of any feelings of joy? Mostly, aside from the pain and the rage, I'm okay being sick. If I was like *her* before I was the way I am now, I probably did the same: worried so much about what I didn't want to happen that I couldn't worry about what was already happening. What if I was so inattentive that I couldn't recognize the things that were happening that I *wanted* to happen?

I feel like I'm forgetting about something though—how long have I been eating? Where's the—where's the man? The shotgun racks. I snap my head towards the decisive sound coming from over my left shoulder, and see a gun barrel pointed at me just out of my reach—my back should've been against the wall. I say "wait," because the only thing that everyone wants is more time, but of course it's verbalized as only a mouth-filled groan—I regrettably lose some food too as a couple pieces of the woman fall to the floor. "Will?" The man said a word at me, and his voice sounds different than before. "Will, what…Will, can you understand me?" The gun is still too far away from me to grab it, even though the man is crouched with one knee on the floor, but I can throw some of the woman at him and buy myself an opportunity to eat him too; and the child, I can see it, in the other corner of the room behind him—both of them perfect. Both of them plagued by perfection. The man said words at me and now his face looks different, he looks like he might not shoot again—he said "Will" like that should've meant something to me. I'm eating the woman he came in with, and he's saying words at me. Does he think that he knows me? I barely know me. Maybe that's how it is: people think they know you because they knew you, even if the person you were isn't the person you are; even if the person you used to be is dead. People infect people. Maybe I already made him sick in a different way, that must be why the man has water falling from his face. "You know who I am, right? You, you still recognize me, don't you? Will, it's me—it's me, Omar. *Omar.*" I throw the food I have in my hand at his face and the gun goes off—*BANG!*—"Ahh!" A high-pitched scream is thrown from the child's mouth. The man racks the gun again—*BANG!* —nothing hits me; racks again—*CLICK.* Aside from the small clicking sound and the child whimpering in the corner, there's silence. I am the pain, I am the rage, I am everything I don't want. I am the ferocious stray dogs inside of me that have nearly killed each other for a meal that they never had the chance to finish, and now they're more consumed by ferocity than ever. I lunge at the man and he swings the long-barreled gun at me, it connects with my head but it's light—more of a strong gust of wind than a swift blow with a blunt instrument —so I throw my right hand at his face and feel as my fingernails, like sharp, brown, rusted screws, carve jagged channels into his skin. He yells in agony then angrily asks where the hell I am, but I don't tell him because I assume, by the question, that his sight has been impaired by my counterattack. "It's gonna be okay, pretty girl, alright? Daddy's right here and you're okay." An odd thing for the man to say when the situation is clearly not going well for either of them at all, but, they must need something to believe in that makes them feel better, even if they know it's not true. They must want it even if the only thing it provides them with is the illusion of security. "Do you hear me, Kennedy? Tell me that you hear me, *please*." In between words the man is swinging the gun back and forth erratically, seemingly without rhythm, but if chaos ensues for long enough even it can develop something resembling a pattern. I dive at him right as he is beginning to cock-back for another go round, and tackle him onto his back. The man yells, the child screams, I bite a large piece of his face off, and he drops the gun to use both of his hands to stop the bleeding. I grab his hand that's nearest to me, lock as many fingers as I can between my teeth, and tear them off—I don't hear anything anymore, not anything specific, just a swirl of noise, like putting large seashells from the beach over both of my ears. I slam the man's head on the floor until it cracks open; he finally stops yelling—his mouth stops moving, anyway—and I can finally eat again in peace.

I think I've been eating for awhile—it must've been awhile —because there isn't much left of the man and the woman, and I don't see the child in the room anymore, but I can hear it crying somewhere—it's still in the house. I stand up, and some of the man—or woman—falls out of the opening by my ribs and lands on the floor. Just laying there it looks like such a waste, but I don't have anymore space for it—I know that's why it fell out to begin with. At one point, that could've been pieces of me on the floor, but it wasn't me, and it isn't me because I'm sick. The worst thing that could've happened to me is keeping me from being someone's food. The worst thing that could've happened to me isn't looking so bad, now that the part I was scared of is over. The child is still crying, I can hear it. It's afraid because something it didn't want to happen has happened. It's afraid because things have changed. It's afraid because it's alone. It might even be afraid because it thinks that something they don't want to happen is about to happen to them again, and they have no idea when, and it could even be worse than what's already happened. But, the child knows nothing, just like the man and the woman. No one knows if what they consider to be the worst possible outcome will end up being the precise catalyst they need the most[2].

I am going to find the child now.

---

[2] *The Catalytic Principle:* Neither right nor wrong exist, there are only catalysts and non-catalysts. Either a person, action, or situation causes change, or it does not. Whether the catalysts are viewed as positive or negative is a perspective of one's own invention to more easily compartmentalize the way in which they are affected.

THE UNDEAD EYE: KENNEDY

I can see that I'm different from a lot of the others, I'm smaller than they are. We're all sick, but they're bigger than I am and I don't know why. I don't think that it really changes anything, and it doesn't seem to matter in any way that I can see, it's just something I've noticed. I think people say words at me more—the people that aren't sick—and I think it's because I'm smaller. The people seem to be more okay around things that are smaller than they are. I see the bigger people with other small people like me who aren't sick, and they're always holding their hands. They say words at them differently, usually softer than they say at the bigger people, and give them things more often too. The smaller people have to be carried a lot, and I *never* see the smaller people carrying anything, yet the bigger people do much more for the smaller people than they do for the other bigger people. It's like the less people think you can do for yourself, the more people want to do for you—regardless of what it costs them. And you can always tell which person people think can do a lot for themselves, because they want that person to do a lot for *everyone*, and still not have anyone to do extra things for them. They break down their strongest, raise up their weakest, and then do it all over again. I don't get it, but that's just how I've seen the people who aren't sick do things. No one does anything for me though. When you're sick, you do everything for yourself—it doesn't matter how big or small you are. It doesn't matter how much you can't carry or how slow you move—you do everything for yourself when you're sick or nothing gets done at all. All I have is me, and the only help I have is my own. Honestly, I've gotten used to it. Being as small as I am actually helps me because then the bigger people always ask "Can I help you, little girl?"— especially when there's no one else around like me who's sick. They just walk right up to me, and say words at me, and get really close, and I don't say *anything*, I just wait and try not to let them see my face. My face scares the people because some of it fell off. I didn't want it to fall off, but it just did. When they see my face then they *know* I'm sick, and then they change how they say words at me, and their face changes too. Some people point guns at me, try to hit me with things, or throw things at me, and I don't like any of that. From what I see, I don't eat as much as the others that are sick, so most times I just want to be left alone, but the people still get mad at me because I'm sick, and they do things that I don't like. I don't care that they're *not sick*, but they care that *I am*. I don't even have to try to bite them or eat them for them to do things to me that I don't like—I didn't choose to be sick. The people don't like me because I'm not like them, even though I didn't ask to be different. Then I stop liking them because they don't like me. And I'll do things that *they* don't like to them because they did things to me first that *I* didn't like. If you're different from someone in a way that makes them feel good about themselves, they'll pity you, but if you're different in any other way, they'll hate you. I should be scared of the people because I'm sick, because they hate *everyone* that's sick. They hate me for being what I am even though I can't change that now—they can change though. I don't even know why I care what the people think, because if my face looked the same as the other small people who aren't sick, then the bigger people who aren't sick would say soft words at me even once they saw how I looked. It's not fair. Just because you know how something looks, doesn't mean you know what something is. This is why I hate them and they make me so mad inside. Anyone can get sick, and I've never seen anyone who was sick go back to not being sick, so the same people that find it so easy to hate me could end up just like me. If it takes someone being *like* me for them to like me, I hope we never have anything in common. Or maybe that's not true. Maybe it doesn't matter *why* people like you, just as long as they can find a reason to. I wish I didn't feel so alone all of the time—I wish I didn't feel so different. There isn't even anyone I can talk to about how I feel because no one cares, and on top of that, no one understands me.

It's getting dark now, and I wish that it wasn't—bad things happen in the dark. Something about the dark makes things different, makes *people* different. During the day the sun shines on some places, and doesn't shine on others—there's a balance. At night the balance is lost and all that remain are the shadows, then everywhere becomes somewhere to hide. When people can hide what they do where it can't be seen, that's when they do what they really want. That's when they can do the things that no one would ever want the light to see. I hear the bad things happening to other people, so I just try to make sure that nothing bad happens to me. I don't even know why I'm here, or if I should be here at all—I could've died instead of just getting sick, and I don't know why I didn't. I don't know why someone who was sick didn't just kill me and eat me, the way that I see them kill and eat people everyday and every night. The same way that they're doing right now—I can hear them. That could be me that someone else was listening to right now. The noises sound like a trail of bread crumbs from a half-remembered nightmare. The more I try not to listen, the clearer the path becomes, and pieces of a reality that doesn't sound fair or nice for anyone all fall into place. I guess if things aren't fair for anyone then they're also fair for everyone.

BANG! The loud boom makes my shoulders instinctively shoot up towards my ears, like a hand raising to answer a question. I'm not scared, I just don't like loud sounds like that one, and I can tell that it's not far away. A lot of the others that are like me like the loud sounds. They like them because they know that means there are people near by, and that means there's something to eat. People make a lot of noise when they're scared, it's almost like they need someone else to know how they feel—as if *sharing* how frightened they are will make the situation less frightening. I can see two people that are sick walking past my home right now in the direction that the sound came from. I hope there won't be more noise soon—I'm going to stay in my home.

I don't know how many other people that are sick have homes, so I like that I was able to find one. It's just a car, but I like it. It doesn't look very nice on the outside—most of it's rusty, and it doesn't have any wheels or a top for the trunk—but I think it's nice on the inside. A nice inside is better than a nice outside, but I don't think everyone knows that. I think no one tries to come in here because of how the outside looks, and that's fine with me. I know it's not really a "home", and I know it's not really "mine", but it still feels like home to me. Anywhere can feel like home if you want it to be. *BANG!* My shoulders move up again, and I can hear them now—the people—they're coming this way. There's a mirror on the outside of my home that's cracked in a way that makes the glass splinter like a spider's web; if I want to see things that are going on outside without going outside, I usually use this one because I like how it makes things look funny. I ease myself closer to the mirror, and move my head and eyes around until I'm in the right place to see behind the car— *BANG!* I duck away quickly and shrink down to the floor of the front seat. People are running this way, and people that are sick are chasing them. I slowly bring myself up from the floor, through the space where a steering wheel should be, and peak into my mirror again. There are three girls frantically running as fast as they can, their hair of different lengths swaying and bouncing with their movements—all of them bigger people—and one of them, one of the girls has a smaller person, like my size, clinging to them tightly. The smaller person has their face pressed into the girl's neck, and their arms clasped around her like a necklace.

"Maria, I can't keep running like this with him! We have to hide somewhere!" The smaller person is getting carried, and the girl carrying it can barely hold on—I don't even know what it would feel like to be carried. "Where could we possibly hide?! We're in the goddamn forest!" The girl with the gun said that—she's the noisemaker—she stops, spins around, and fires three quick shots—*BANG! BANG! BANG!* The closest sick person to her is hit twice, causing them to stumble and fall, and they're passed by four others who are still coming after the girls. "Bree, look! C'mon, Maria!" The girl who is carrying neither a gun or a person says this; it gets the attention of the girl holding the weapon, and she resumes running with the others. Oh no, no this isn't good—they're pointing, and they're pointing right at my home! I don't know what to do, no one ever tries to come in here, and there's three of them and they're scared. When people are scared and they have weapons, someone usually gets hurt, and I don't want to get hurt again. I go back to my hiding place in the front seat and do the only thing I can think of—wait.

"Okay, so now what?" I can't tell which one of them said that. All of them are outside at the front of the car, but I can only see the tops of their heads through the window. "What do you mean, 'Now what?' Leena, it's your turn to shoot—hurry up. Is Donnie okay?" I really wish I could see what they're doing. "Yeah, he looks okay. Hey, Don-Don, you doing okay? Yeah, he's a big boy." Don-Don must be the smaller person, because the girl changed how she said words at him. "Okay, good. Jesus Christ, Neleena, *please* start shooting these things!" *Shooting* means more noise—of course. "*Okay*, okay. You know I hate this!" *BANG! BANG!* I stay as low as I can and crawl between the two front seats and make my way into the back. The gun is very loud and I *hate* that sound, just like the girl said—maybe she's like me. *BANG! BANG! BANG!* "It's okay, Donnie, you're okay, you're okay—Maria, *please* tell me some good news." The sick people are closer now, I can clearly hear them groaning, so they can't be too far away from the car. "Ay, I need you to reload it, quick! I'm not gonna be fast enough." *BANG!* "Shit, Leena, lemme see it before you're all…okay—never mind." I don't think the girls have been keeping a good look out. Two sick people are walking past the rear passenger-side window, and I'm still on the floor, as low as I can be. One of the sick people sees me through the window, gives me the slightest nod, and continues to walk towards the front of the car with the other sick person behind him. "Ahhh! Leena, Maria—help!" A sick person must have got her—"Take Donnell, quick! Donnie, go! Go!"—and she sounds like she's only worried about whether the smaller person is safe or not. "Leena, grab her fast! I'm almost done!" Another sick person is walking past the passenger-side—"Nooo! Leena, pull harder!"—that doesn't sound good. "I'm trying! Let her go, you monster! Maria, hurry—" *BANG! BANG!* "Arrrgh" *BANG! BANG! BANG!* Sounds like she was able to shoot someone—"There's more coming!"—but she'll need to shoot a few more. "Everyone in the car! We can hold 'em off from inside there! Quick!" Oh no, no they can't come in here, this is *my home*, and I'm sick, and they hate everyone that's sick—what do I do?! The door is opening. I'll hide my face and then maybe they'll just want to help me. "Get in, get in, get in!" *BANG! BANG!* The girl holding the smaller person sits in the passenger seat in front of me, the other girl sits beside her and closes the door; the girl with the gun is opening the back door and drops down beside me—even though it's dark, *I* have no where to hide. "Oh my God! There's a kid in here?!" I can hear the other two girls in the front turning to look back at me, so I make sure my hands are covering as much of my face as they can— being yourself can get you in a lot of trouble. "Is she okay?"

Two more sick people are at the back windows now, one on each side of the car, I can hear them banging. "Hey, is she okay or not? Because we got friends at the door, and they look hungry!" I hope they don't hate me. "She's a child by *herself*; gimme a second. Hello there, little one. My name is Maria, and this is Neleena and Breeanne. I'm going to help you over to one of them, okay? Then I can get rid of the bad people outside. Is that okay with you?" I nod my head. Maybe not all people are the same, maybe if you give people a chance to be better, they actually will be. "Okay, good. Give me your hand and I'll help you to the front." My back is still facing her and my face is covered, so I twist slightly to my left and remove my left hand from my face to reach out towards her. My hands are pretty small, so with only one of them covering my face, if the people were scared of me, they would've already—"Jesus! Maria, don't *touch it!* It's face is falling off! It's sick! Shoot the ones outside *and* this thing!" Or, maybe if you give people a chance to be better, they'll show you that there's no such thing. I move my hand back to my face to cover it up. One of the sick people outside hits the window hard enough that it cracks. "We don't have time for this! What are you waiting for?!" I part my fingers just enough to see who's yelling, and it's the bigger person with no gun or smaller person with them; I could do something to her that she wouldn't like, just like she's doing to me. "Maria, listen to Leena or don't, but do something about the ones *out there!* We have Donnie." I don't like the one who was yelling, I wish the sick people got her—I could get her if I wanted to. "Sorry, Bree, you're right. Hey, little one, can you come closer to me? Because the windows are gonna break and glass will go all over. We don't want you getting hurt, okay?" I like this bigger person, her words are very soft. I still keep my face covered and don't turn around, I just inch my way back like a caterpillar one small movement at a time. "You *can't* be serious?! Look at her!" The bigger person that I don't like snaps her hand closed around my arm like a lobster claw, and yanks it away from my face; I yell "it's not my fault," but no words come out, only the ugly groans. There are few things more fatal to who you are than being misunderstood. I see the face of the nicer, bigger person become like everyone else's who hates me—I bite into the arm of the one that grabbed me. This is her fault, but I know that won't make a difference. She pulls her arm away screaming, the bigger person holding the smaller person is screaming too, and I can feel the moist blood and flesh on my face and tongue. The bigger person holding the gun isn't making any noise at all, she's just pointing the gun at me. I tried my best, but my best wasn't good enough. *BANG!*

THE UNDEAD EYE: DR. GREN

T his wasn't supposed to happen to me—ever. My name is Dr. Emmalene Gren, and I can no longer speak. I volunteered myself for quarantine as a safety precaution because I don't know when my thoughts will no longer be my own. My colleagues have tried to reassure me that our work is not in vain, and that they will find a cure in time to save me—the sentiment is appreciated, but I haven't lost my memory yet. I know what I'm up against.

It's my fault that I'm like this now, it's my fault that I'm sick and will soon be another one of the mindless zombies that some of us are trying to cure, and others are trying to eradicate. We're not supposed to use the term "zombie", but we all know that's what they are. I know that's where this one-way street is heading for me, and there's no turning back now that I'm on it. To some, acceptance appears to be the same as surrender, but I'm confident that the two are merely siblings, not identical twins. I will fight this, but I will also be realistic.

My proximity to the subject in question wasn't what it should've been. I got too close, I got reckless, and now I'm paying for it. She was the first child with the infection that I've ever seen; just a little girl with her neck and head hanging maybe three inches away from falling off of her shoulders when…she grabbed me. It was unbelievable. Her battered little hand attached itself to my arm before I could blink. Each one of her fingernails tore into my skin like a harpoon through a marlin, and now I'm here, quarantined.

There aren't many who know as well as I do how MANDSS (Muscular and Neural Degenerative Suspension Syndrome; also called Odulé's Disease) is contracted, how it progresses, and how it completely takes over. I should've been more careful, but I was more concerned with the *job* than my safety. More than anything I wanted to make a difference—*want* to make a difference—and because of that, I pushed harder than I should've. I've always known that progress requires sacrifice, and that most aren't willing to lose what brings them comfort in order to gain what's necessary for success—apparently I'm not "most people". Lucky me.

We've all heard the story—more legend now than anything else—of how the neurologist, Dr. Desmond Odulé, made the unfortunate initial discovery of the infection while on vacation with his wife, Gina, and infant daughter in Australia. Approximately 16 hours after Gina lost her speech, Dr. Odulé woke up to his wife of four years sitting on the sun-soaked deck of their rental home with her face covered in fresh blood, holding the severed left arm of their daughter—that's all that was left of her. I'm currently on my fourth hour, still 12 left until I'm likely to lose control of my cognitive functions, but not all of those around me are optimistic about my current state or possible recovery. They haven't told me directly, they just whisper loud enough for me to overhear. To them hour 16 is irrelevant, I'm already a statistic, just another sad case: a human being who's no longer human. I've always found it interesting how we cling to the imaginary lines of normalcy as if they were life itself, and since this pandemic began, it's become even less of a substantial concept to me. Normalcy is a line drawn in the sand, and each time the tide rises and washes it away, it's never redrawn in quite the same place as it was before. Of course, I never realized how perfectly ridiculous it was until now, now that something so subjective is separating me from everything and everyone I know. Now that I'm on the "wrong side" of normal. Odulé came to mind because he was there, he was there the whole time, and he witnessed the entire transformation in the worst way possible. I wonder how he could've possibly maintained such an excruciatingly high level of optimism? (Prior to his suicide, naturally). Seeing what's happening but not knowing why or how and then, regrettably, holding on to a dream long enough for it to erupt into a nightmare, and then to spawn something even worse. There's a very real, and very fine line between optimism and negligence—I rather not be on the wrong side of *that line* either.

Hour seven: I reported that I was experiencing some abdominal discomfort and I was given a CT scan to be on the safe side—nine of my organs have shut down. Nine. And all I felt was what amounted to a nagging stomachache, I've had the same one before after eating too much candy on Halloween. I'm as nervous as I am intrigued. For me to suffer organ failure of that magnitude, and basically feel nothing, is unparalleled, and obviously not in a good way. If my team doesn't attempt to cut off the progression of the infection, they can track its entire development. They may not be able to cure me, but with the data that they collect, they may be able to cure every known carrier, and possibly assemble a preventative vaccine. Everything we undoubtedly know about MANDSS, we've had to reconstruct from dead or dying subjects—well, subjects who were dead or dying *again*—so to have me is...a dream really—scientifically speaking. I can be the GPS that displays the route that the infection takes, so I may be the best opportunity that we have of accomplishing something that truly helps people. I also don't want to become one of the people that needs help, but I guess I've already cut the ribbon as far as that's concerned. We hope to never be in a situation where we require the same assistance that we offer to others, but in many ways, that's the only way to understand what it is that we offer at all.

I get it now, as I desperately try to remember what day it is. I get it: I have no options, and I'm at the mercy of those who wield them—I can only hope that they decide in a way that I find favorable. I don't want to die, more importantly, I don't want to witness losing everything that makes me who I am, that would be like being buried alive, in which case, I would opt for the literal version. I legitimately don't know what day it is though, it could be Tuesday, or...Tues...day? Or...Christ, I, I don't know what other days there are—how can I *not* know this?!

"Hey, how are you?" It's Macy, Macy Roper, she came to see me! Finally, a friendly face—I wonder why she hadn't come sooner? It's been more than three hours since she was last here. This time she has a moderately flat, white box with her—maybe take-out from a restaurant. I open my mouth to speak, quickly remember what the outcome would be, and immediately bite my tongue. Maybe four hours ago I tried saying something out loud, just to myself, and what escaped from my mouth was a cringe-inducing groan. I sounded like a bear wounded by a hunter's bow, wailing in agony. Hearing that once is plenty. I pick up my phone from the small food tray that's attached to the hospital-style bed, open a text message to Macy, type her my response, get up to walk over to the glass partition she's standing on the other side of, and hold up my phone so she can read it: "Thank God you're back! Hey, I'm trying not overreact in here, and I know it's best I be here, but please tell me you have good news!" She leans closer to the glass and reads the message. She smiles sheepishly at the screen before addressing me.

"You know I wish I did, Emma, seriously, but just with protocol and everything, I mean, you know how it is with..." She shrugs and lets her sentence trail off; I write her back.

"SUBJECTS, right, I know how it is with subjects. Of course. You're absolutely right."

"We went and got pizza. I convinced them to at least let me bring you some real food. It's just pepperoni." Macy looks up at the small camera overhead that's facing where she's standing, and innocently lifts the box up chest-high towards it. I can't help but to smile at her with every ounce of perceivable happiness that I'm able to extract. Macy's the best friend that your Mom prayed you'd meet on the first day of preschool. I text her again: "I really don't deserve you, Macy."

"Jesus, Emma, it's just pizza."

We both laugh and she unlocks the small, air-tight compartment to her right, places the personal-sized square box of pizza into it, and reseals the door. I mouth "thank you" from the other side of the glass, and shape my hands into a makeshift heart and hold it to my chest. She blows me an exaggerated kiss in return, waves, and proceeds down the hallway away from my room. I unlock and open the separate air-tight compartment door on my end, and I can't remember ever being more thrilled by the distinctive aroma of greasy mozzarella cheese, tomato sauce, and processed meat—this is what love smells like. I've never believed that the best things in life were free, but I could be convinced that they don't cost as much as I thought they did. I flip the top of the box up to dive in but pause—based on the grease mark, there's clearly a slice that's missing. In the space where the second slice of pizza should be, there's a folded napkin with Macy's handwriting on it: "They ran tests and they need more data. I'm SO sorry, Emma." If they need more data that means they need more time, and time's the one thing I can't spare. My execution papers have been signed. Closing the pizza box, I walk back over to the bed, put the box on the tray, climb into bed and pull the thin, papery sheets up to my neck—lunch can wait. The pizza box is mocking me. It's never even been alive, but it was the messenger that informed me of my death —ironic. Regardless, I'm giving it a death stare although I'd like to set the box on fire. There are rules against shooting the messenger, but I've never heard anything about burning it. Macy couldn't have told me, I'm sure she wanted to but she couldn't, not with the camera there. We can only use our work phones while in the building, so anything she sent me would have been accessible by the company—this grim reaper of a pizza box was chosen instead. I'd like to say that I "deserve better", but I know that's not true. No one deserves to have anything done the way they desire it—that's a gift, a miracle worthy of celebration.

Hour 10: I've wanted to work on infectious diseases ever since I was...ever since...well, I'm having trouble remembering the exact age, but it was since I was fairly young. It's difficult to accurately describe how thoroughly aggravating it is not being able to recall simple facts. Imagine tapping the outside of your pocket and feeling that your keys are inside, but when you reach in to grab them nothing's there. It's like that. Now look at me, I've spent the majority of my adult life fighting against infections, now the infection and I are one. Has it always been this way and I just never took the time to notice? That what we *fight* and what we *are* stand shoulder to shoulder; that we fight what we fight against because a part of us knows that in an instance we could be one and the same.

I'm obnoxiously hungry right now. The pizza has long since lost it's fragrant aroma, but it's still sitting on the tray in front of me in it's smug cardboard box. I hate this evil box, yet I'm trying to decide if I'd like to throw it across the room, or pull it closer to me. I don't feel good. I haven't been able to sleep. I've never felt so exhausted in my entire life, but when I close my eyes nothing happens, and I've never had trouble sleeping. *I love sleep*. Maybe I'm not hungry, maybe this thing

I'm feeling in my stomach isn't hunger at all, but another sign that a different part of me is shutting down. It could be both, and if it is, then eating something would at least be moving in a helpful direction. If I *believe* it will help, maybe I can convince my body that it actually will. The Placebo Effect is amazing in that way. A seemingly simple change in mentality manifesting itself physically—it's Macy's favorite. She once told me that what we believe will always be more powerful than what's real—I've never hoped that she was right more than I do right now.

Hour 15: I don't know why I was in that bed for so long when I knew I couldn't sleep. I'm pacing now, as best I can, because it helps me think. I don't know if I should be keeping my mind active or quiet, so I'm opting for what I'm used to: active. I can no longer feel my toes on my right foot—no pain, no tingling, just no feeling at all. So walking feels different, like picking up a glass with my left hand instead of my right, and raising it to my mouth in order to drink—it just doesn't feel familiar. The pacing has helped though because I've realized something: none of this was coincidental, it was a set up. They gave me that patient on purpose. They gave me that poor little girl to examine, and they knew I would get too close, and they *knew* this would happen—Macy and I always talked about wanting to have little girls of our own. Macy! I can't believe it! I don't know how I haven't I seen this the entire time: it was her all along! She must have told them and had them put me in there with that patient just so I could get sick, and then they could all have their live specimen to watch disintegrate. Her closing thematic gesture was bringing me that note to let me know I was dead, and then strutting away laughing—she must be so goddamn proud of herself. She must be the belle of the ball, dancing away in her golden dress with all of the bastards who wanted this. They're *evil* people. They're worse than the zombies. They're worse than *I am*. God, I hate them. God, I...or—or is this MANDSS? Is this its final brush stroke smeared over the last clean corner of my mind? Is this...*NO! What the hell is wrong with me?!* No, I see exactly what this is! And I'm one hundred percent justified in being the most *horribly* revolted that I've ever been, because this, this out of *all* possible circumstances will probably be my last recognized experience with humanity: lied to and deceived—how uniquely human. The easiest lie for people to tell is the one that hides something they're ashamed of, I suppose that's how she fooled me so gracefully[3].

I've never felt such pure anger build within me before. Maybe I should eat something to calm myself down, and at least try to fight it. I walk back over to the bed tray, place one hand on either side of the flimsy cardboard box, open it, pick up the cold pizza and take three big bites—it tastes like nothing at all; not like cheese, or dough, or sauce, or anything. If I wasn't holding it in my hand right in front of my face, I would've thought that I just bit into plastic—but even that tastes like *something*. This isn't right. On the opposite side of the bed there's a short, generic side table with a small bouquet of mixed flowers. I walk over to it, get close, and inhale deeply—nothing. Taste and smell, both gone—this is really happening. Today. I pick up the flowers and throw them as hard as I can towards the glass partition

---

[3] *Falsehood Theory:* A lie is the truth had circumstances been different. It's a believable alternative to a provable fact or sincere point of view, so all that really separates a lie from the truth is a thorough imagination. In essence, lies and truths are in the same category—they're both stories one chooses to accept or deny.

that separated me and Macy. I walk back over to the pizza box, pick it up and do the same. The pizza falls out and lands on the floor, and I'm so hungry that I move as quickly as I can to get to it, pick it up, and tear through every piece. It does nothing—I need something, something *fresher*—even once I've chewed and swallowed all of it, it's like I never had it to begin with. What a metaphor for my dismal situation: I've lived only a fraction of my life, only for it to be devoured like it never existed. Not exactly how I planned on spending my birthday.

BEWARE

The Titans are killing us all, and I feel powerless in the wake of the destruction—they must feel powerless as well. Those without power or purpose in their own lives are the first to seek power and dominion over the lives of others. I pray that death overcomes me before the inclination to become like my enemy does. To become like them would be the voluntary act of choosing to be a plague upon our environment. I would be pledging myself as an agent of imbalance and disruption, like an oil spill with an agenda—how the Titans have survived so long and so mightily in this manner is baffling, to say the least. Some of those in the hive—both male Maters and female Maintainers—have chosen to dedicate their entire lives to the study of the Titans' tendencies, psychology, and sociology. One such dedicated being is my closest younger male sibling, Weijia, who is startlingly brilliant. It was the theory he researched, and the data he recorded and published, which first provided our hive with tangible answers regarding rumors that the flora and vegetation we'd pollinated for centuries was now taking our lives. Truthfully, even I was skeptical until I saw it for myself, and then I had no choice but to obey what my eyes were telling me. I didn't want to lose the familiarity of tradition, nor the ease of the habitual. It's tradition and habit that form so much of the ground we stand on, but once they're removed, standing is no longer an option—we must learn to fly. We must face our fear of the fall in order to create a favorable future. At its most persuasive fear is paralyzing, and it's hard to walk—let alone fly—when you're paralyzed.

"This is it, Arlen, this is where it all became clear to me." Although I'd never been, I'd heard of this particular field and that it was one of the mating congregation areas of a nearby hive, and often visited by the Maintainers as well for pollination. It was the middle of the day and the sun hung almost directly overhead amidst a soft, cloudless coat of blue sky. As I flew away from Weijia's side, below me were deep, green leaves and vegetation on the ground in varying stages of roundness, reflecting colors of both bright orange and green with orange splashes—it all seemed as it should be.

"Weijia! Are you sure this is the place? Everything here seems perfectly—"

"Don't!" I've never regarded my younger male sibling as much of an accomplished flyer, but he was off and immediately next to me just as quickly as I'd seen in any of our stealthier counterparts. "*Don't*—don't touch anything. Everything you can see *might* kill you, but everything you *can't* absolutely will. This place may be aesthetically inviting, but the Titans have layered it with toxins that will shutdown your brain in less than one Sun movement." I hover above the deep, golden-yellow flower that I was one small motion away from landing on. Its petals extend out in five separate directions like broad sunrays, as if it were a miniature reflection of the light giver it opens itself up to and reaches towards for rejuvenation—this, according to Weijia, could've killed me. How regrettable it is when that which creates life and beauty in the world can be used to create the exact opposite, yet, how shortsighted one must be to assume that one creation holds more value than the other—these two rival thoughts often leave me divided.

"But, what about the Titans? We all know that they touch and ingest these same fruit, and I imagine they aren't poisoning *themselves*."

"Isn't it funny how at times our imaginations cannot imagine what is already a reality? For reasons I have yet to discover, sadly you're wrong. They *are* poisoning themselves. Now, does it affect and kill them as swiftly as it does with us? It doesn't, but, from the tests that my team have run to validate my suspicions, what they've covered this vegetation with is poisonous to all who ingest it. The poison just reacts in different ways depending on the animal. I'm sure the Titans' size assists with their longevity." If I wasn't hearing this directly from Weijia, I would've assumed that what I was being told was either a purposeful deception or grossly misunderstood, but it was obviously neither.

"So they would kill themselves just to kill us?"

"Not only us, remember, *countless* other insects are affected as well, but, the short answer is yes, yes they would, and they are."

"But, don't they know that our work benefits them?"

"I can't say for sure. I would think that with their apparent intelligence that they must know, yes, but then if they did, how could they justify putting our lives in danger? I don't know."

I knew there had been more reports than usual of Maintainers going out for pollination flights and never returning. As I had become increasingly more involved in community organizing within the hive, I did my best to help those who were closest to the ones that perished, and *I* witnessed the impact—the disbelief, the confusion, the fear.

Moving forward was never a straight line. Calamity—particularly the type that involves the loss of life—can inspire an array of emotions and outlooks that sadden, or uplift, but all are valid. Prior to Weijia's examinations, when all that we understood was based on hearsay, there were already those who were ready for rash action to be taken. Some questioned why we didn't attack the Titans by uniting all of the hives willing to defend their families and simply overwhelm them with our numbers—a suicide mission, of course, for the Maintainers who would fight for us all; intending to solve death by going on the offensive against it. Others, like the voices who initially inspired Weijia himself, wanted to know how information could be gathered and provided to those with the honor and responsibility of pollinating, in order for them to remain safe enough to make it back home alive. Discovering the exact cause of the danger or why it had developed wasn't what they were primarily concerned with; intending to solve death by going on the defensive. Naturally, for many, the *reason* behind these critical developments was their primary point of interest. If the work of the Maintainers outside of the hive had mutated into a position that was undeniably more deadly than it had been previously, discovering the cause of the mutation was paramount and could lead to crucial insight on how to proceed. They intended to solve death by understanding it. Lastly, there was a point of view—veering away from Authorist Futurism[4]—that arose from the hive members who lived for the dead,

---

[4] Authorist Futurism: An Authorist acknowledges that the only thing ahead of them is a blank canvas. They believe the composition to fill that canvas is decided by nothing short of what they want for themselves, their will and determination to create it, and their readiness to see that what they intended may have taken on a different form, and presented a progressive opportunity that they could not have previously foreseen. Authorist Futurism encapsulates vision, action, and fluidity.

and who couldn't handle the trauma of loss. They were choked in a cloud of dismay and inhaled the harsh, blistering smoke of demoralization which impregnated them and gave birth to hopelessness—what could be done? The Maintainers had no choice but to continue pollinating until a solution was found, and as the rumors spread like bacteria, so did the Surrenderist Futurism[5] attitude of "it is what it is." As far as they were concerned, normalcy now had a new face, and although they didn't recognize it the only option was to familiarize themselves. They intended to solve death by quietly accepting it. Once Weijia brought his findings back to our family, everyone found something in his material that supported their line of thinking. In a way it helped as much as it hindered.

Weijia nudges me.

"You good?"

"Yeah—sorry—I'm fine, it's just—"

"A lot to wrap your head around, right?"

"Yeah…yeah, I guess that's what it is."

"I have one more place to show you. It'll be quick." I know enough about my sibling to know that any sentence ending with "it'll be quick" refers to something that certainly won't be, but *will* most likely be interesting. I take one last look at the field of invisible execution, and let Weijia know that wherever we're going needs to mathematically not take long —I'm dying to get something to eat.

---

[5] Surrenderist Futurism: A Surrenderist accepts that their present forecasted the unalterable events of their future, so that consequently, they would surrender to said forecasted outcome presuming they could no longer affect it—the Surrenderist encapsulates hope, inaction, and acceptance.

We end up at a large field across from an undisturbed playground, and like the vegetation patch we just left, nothing appears out of the ordinary at first glance. Lush, green grass covers the field on either side of a paved walkway—the left side is adorned with small, white, unopened flowers scattered across it, while the right side is bare. Once the pronounced contrast is noticed, I'm nervous about what it may reveal; Weijia flies ahead of me and indicates that I should follow. When he finally slows the buzzing of his wings and lands on one of the Titan's wooden resting posts, he directs my attention to an area of hard, artificial soil beneath us, and I'm immediately possessed by a demon of intense nausea. Three members of the hive are on the ground—two clearly dead, one moving so slowly it's like there's a force physically pulling them in the opposite direction of where they're trying to go.

"What's wrong with them, Weijia? Can we help *her?*"

"I'm not sure what's wrong with them. And no, we haven't determined how to help yet—we're still working on what exactly the Titans have done to this place."

"Is it painful?"

"They aren't able to communicate once they're exposed. The poison must attack that part of the brain first—attack their ability to express anything—but that's just a guess. For the time being, I've just been having the information circulated as much as possible to stay away from here." It was horrible. I almost wished he hadn't brought me, but I know that my willful ignorance wouldn't be of any aid to those at the hive who I could help. It's situations like these that make it incredibly difficult to remember and utilize the ideals of the hive. Instilled within us all is the doctrine that good and evil don't exist—the teachings of The Catalytic Principle[6] are explicitly clear—that positive and negative are not inherent, but perspectives of our own invention. This is the wisdom I must cling to now tighter than I have at any time previously. What has happened to so many others, and what is happening to these Maintainers at this moment, is simply a catalyst causing a change—things are changing, and we must adjust accordingly.

"Why is only the left side of the field flowered?"

"You really should get out more, Arlen."

"Hilarious. What's wrong with the flowers?"

"The Titans have machines that erase them."

" 'Machines'? They kill flowers? *Flowers?*"

"They'll be here soon to finish off the rest of them as well, that much I'm sure of." I say nothing, I just stare at the mutilated area where life was set to bloom. What's there to say about animals who premeditate the extermination of flowers? "Hey, I know how this looks. We're obviously akin to an environment of balance, but the Titans know no balance—if they weren't tipping the scales, they may have no place on them at all. They're the alpha species of this planet, and they're only growing more devious in their methods of survival." Suddenly I'm aware of my own chest rising and falling, and the low, droning vibration from my wings that hum in the key of motion throughout my entire body. The wind blows through the leaves of the trees above me playing the same soothing, swaying song as ocean waves against the seashore. It's an understated similarity that I never took notice of before now, and an immersing reminder that all is

---

[6] The Catalytic Principle: Neither right nor wrong exist, there are only catalysts and non-catalysts. Either a person, action, or situation causes change, or it does not. Whether the catalysts are viewed as positive or negative is a perspective of one's own invention to more easily compartmentalize the way in which they are affected.

connected. "Arlen, I'll be right back, okay?" I nod. Weijia flies down to the three that have been infected and begins taking notes—none of them feel what I'm feeling right now, none of them feel anything at all.

BRRRGGG! A mouthful of sharp, ear-gnawing noise explodes from somewhere behind me—the Titans are here, and they brought their machine with them. Weijia flies back up to where I am—again, quicker than I'd expect from him— and for a split second I see an unfamiliar flash of dread cast a shadow over his face like a waning moon. He displays unrest so infrequently I'm honestly unsure of how to react. It's those who are identified as the strongest, brightest, and bravest who depend most on the support of others, for they are the ones pushing themselves beyond the same internal limits they refuse to acknowledge are in their possession.

"There's nothing we can do, is there?"

"There's one thing: we can get that Maintainer out of the way." Obviously, his eyes are better than mine; it takes me a few seconds, but I spot her just as the machine begins its approach in her direction—*BRRRGGG!* It's so loud we're yelling every word now.

"What's wrong with her?! Something must be wrong!"

"The poison has already hit her! Come on!"

Weijia and I both speed off towards our sibling as fast as we can. The wind blows my antennae back against my face, and I tuck my legs tight against my body to maintain my velocity. Other than the roaring growl of the Titans' machine, all I can hear is the vibratory tone of my wings as I push them to carry me farther faster. The low, steady droning that characterized them only a short time before, is replaced by a higher, more intense buzzing that screams back at me in demonstration for demanding the impossible, and moving without fear of repercussion—we're close now. Synchronized, we dive towards the tops of the grass blades and fly directly towards the Maintainer—*BRRRGGG!*—we have to move quickly to have any chance of pulling this off. She's not far in front of us now, carelessly hovering in a small, irregular circle, as if a monster isn't bearing down upon her.

"All we have to do is get her out of the way! We grab her and keep going!" Weijia's the expert—whatever he thinks we should do, that's what we're doing. I loosen my legs from their previous position and prepare myself for the inevitable impact our maneuver will require—*BRRRGGG!* "Try to time the grab with her flight pattern!" We're only a few seconds away from her now, and we both extend our legs to hook her and get her out of here. "Looks like she's heading your way— let's go!" We both converge to latch on to her, but she's gone! In one quick, spasmodic buzz, she's up and over both our heads. Our momentum causes us to collide and I plummet head first into the dirt.

"Arlen? Arlen?!"

"Yeah! Yeah, I'm over here—I'm good!" *BRRRGGG!* Am I good? Something doesn't feel right with one of my wings and I don't know if I even want to look. It doesn't feel like I can move it, it feels heavy, and it *never* feels heavy. What if—not right now, it can't be—what if it's broken? I may not be feeling any pain due to the adrenaline—I don't want to look, I just don't. I try to move it, but something's holding it back. I can't—I can't move my wing. I take a deep breath—I'm overreacting—I collided with the ground, there's probably just a rock on my wing, and all I need to do is figure out how to get it off.

"Arlen, where are you?! We have to go, now!"

"Alright!" *BRRRGGG!* I get out of my head, compose myself, and finally look back at my wing to assess the damage and get myself out of this. It's mangled, my wing is mangled. A hurricane of panic instantly forms within me, decimating any other reasonable thought that may have existed. My wing is a mass of twisted tree roots, and the sight of it awakens the pain, a monstrous sleeping giant—with rose thorns for teeth—that bites into my nerves. This isn't good.

"Weijia! I might need some help!"

"What?!"

"Help! I need help! I can't fly!" Think—I have to think—there's a way to get out of everything, every time, I just have to find it. *BRRRGGG!*

"Hey, are you o—" His eyes connect with my wing, and I assume he realizes the energy necessary to finish yelling his question would be wasted. "Okay! We'll get you out of the way *first*, then figure out the rest!"

"We have to get her out of here though!"

"And we will! We're dealing with you first!" He signals for me to do something by moving his head around which, in this situation, could mean a few things. Luckily he's my closest sibling, because no one else would be able to understand that he wanted them to roll onto their stomach. He grabs my back legs, "Okay! Here we go!" *BRRRGGG!* He's dragging me, and the Titans' machine is close enough now that if Weijia had his mouth right next to my ear, I wouldn't hear a word over the sound of this monstrosity. We're moving faster than I expected. If this kid has been squeezing in time to work out *and* do all of his science stuff, we can't be related, because…because there's just no way.

The power of the Titans' machine is incredible, it's like nothing I've ever experienced. The entire ground is alive beneath me, violently shaking like it's attempting to defeat gravity, and rip itself off the Earth piece by piece. I can't hold my head still enough for long enough to get my bearings— maybe we haven't moved far at all and this was all pointless. The rumbling continues and continues, and the wind generated from the machine is blowing rocks and pieces of anything that can move in every direction imaginable, but we're still moving, I'm almost sure of it—I hope. Hopefully Weijia's okay, and the Maintainer is still well enough that back at the hive someone on Weijia's team can help her.

"Whoa!" Weijia suddenly places me down and appears directly in front of my eyes.

"Who were you expecting?!"

"Funny! Are you okay?!"

"I'm fine! Are you?!"

"I think so!" My body's on fire, but I want to stand up and see what's going on. We must have gotten pretty far away from the machine, because the drastic shaking isn't as severe.

"Arlen! What are you doing?!" He tries to hold me back, but I move him away with the little energy I have left, and get up tall enough to see through the grass. The machine is close, but it's not coming in our direction—we're actually okay. "Hey, just sit and conserve your energy, because I have no idea yet how we'll all get back to the hive!"

"Who's 'all' ?!"

"I'm going to get her!"

"You won't make it back in time with both of you! Look!" The machine is extremely close to her and she's still hovering in an erratic circle, for all we know, she could have another spasm and fly out of the way. I want to help her, and I want Weijia to get her if he can, but it's not worth two deaths. Weijia may be the only Mater or Maintainer alive who's smart enough to get our hive and the other hives through this—we can't afford to lose him. Sometimes the best move is realizing there aren't any left to be made; and the most heroic option is opting to save one's self.

"I can do it!"

"You can't, Weijia! Actually think about it!" We both look over at the Maintainer. Time is passing incredibly quickly, but her contrasting movements, like a loose leaf caught in a gentle breeze, almost seem to counteract Time's forward motion and slow everything down. She hovers around in another circle, spasms, drifts up, around again and to the right, then immediately drops in a straight line into the grass and out of view.

"NO!" Weijia's in the air before my brain can formulate a reaction to what happened. I watch him as he flies, and he's not as fast as before and barely flying straight. I'm sure having to drag me here took a toll on him. *BRRRGGG!*

"Damnit, Weijia." Without the Maintainer in sight, Time sprints through my mind to make up for the illusion of it's previous slow progression—*BRRRGGG!*—and I can see as Weijia lunges down into the grass to find our poisoned hive member—*BRRRGGG!* All I can do is watch, watch as the Titan and its machine barrel closer and closer to where they are—like watching lightning strike the ground in slow-motion. Yelling is less than useless, even if the machine was silent, the sheer distance would be enough to keep him from hearing me—*BRRRGGG!* It's right on top of them now, and I don't see any yellow and black stripes, like projectiles thrown from a volcanic eruption, triumphantly exploding into the air from the grassy horizon. The machine passes by completely, and still nothing, nothing at all but the colossal roar finally growing softer and shaking the ground less as the machine lumbers into the distance.

As Weijia suggested, I sit down. I sit and I ignore the splitting pain that's desperately trying to hold my attention. I can hear the wind blowing through the trees again, still sounding like the ocean, but now it's Weijia and the Maintainer we tried to save who can no longer hear its song. He's dead—just like that—now what? Now that I've lost someone so close to me, do I crawl my way back to the hive and join the others who are in mourning, and voice my layman's opinion on how we should deal with the tyranny of the Titans? What do you take from monsters who take everything?! I fell into the grass and had to be dragged through it just so I could survive this long—what if *I* was exposed to the poison? What if I'm next to be erased by the Titans?!

"WEIJIA!"

"Yeah?" He's behind me—of course he's behind me— where else could he possibly be? Weijia the Wizard. He drags his feet as he walks to my right, and stands next to me before having a seat, but he's by himself, and he looks the worst I've ever seen him. He's nearly entirely covered in debris, and where there isn't debris, scratches and small wounds are clearly visible. His breathing is labored, he's exhausted, and his eyes are filled with melancholy—I could never picture him being this drained or disappointed. I feel so bad for him it's almost hard to be happy he made it back, because nothing about him says that *he's* even happy he made it back. I tell him I'm sorry, and that he did everything he could have, that he did more than most others could or would have. He sits silently, as do I. After a few minutes, he speaks first. He says the machine will make its way back around to where we're sitting, but he wants to tell me something before we return to the hive. He helps me up and we walk out of the field, across the section of artificial soil, and sit in the grass where the machine has already destroyed the flowers. Weijia informs me why it was so important to rescue that Maintainer before the poison killed her: she would've been perfect to test a hypothesis that he had, and the experiment could only work on someone that had the poison in them, but was still unaffected enough to communicate. Not only does he think exposure to the poison doesn't have to be fatal, there may be a way we could use it to our advantage—just like that, he has a plan. His mind is truly extraordinary.

"So, you can cure this?"

"I think—*think*—that there's a way, yes."

With his head hung low, he goes on to say that for an antidote to be created when the poison is unknown, a sample would be required from that specific carrier. The difficult part would be getting the mandatory amount of blood within the slim window of time when the carrier could be utilized.

"I've done it once, Arlen, but things didn't work out like I'd foreseen. The donor didn't survive the procedure." I know why Weijia wanted to talk to me about this outside of the hive: what he did—and what he was attempting to do again —is illegal. The approval he'd need from the hive to proceed with testing like this wouldn't come quickly, if at all. Additionally, there's the debatable issue of whether or not he's responsible for the death of the donor even though they were likely to die from the poison anyway. Without participating in his procedure, maybe they could've lived a few hours longer.

"But, you were able to save one of them?"

Weijia sighs deeply. "I was, yes, but the procedure wasn't controlled. I was improvising and it was sloppy, but if I didn't act, both of them would've died. What's troubling is that the survivor is displaying symptoms that suggest they'll need another procedure in order to survive any longer."

"Well, I can stay here while you get back to the hive and do what you can for them. Looks like I'm okay here, right?" Weijia pushes himself to stand up, grunting as he makes his way to his feet. He surveys himself and begins to dust off some of the grass and other debris, then stretches his legs and looks over at the distant Titan machine making its way back in our direction.

"The survivor isn't at the hive, Arlen, the survivor is right here. I was hoping to find a donor at the vegetation field, or at this flower field, but if I couldn't find one at either, I needed to make sure I had a donor with me—someone who trusted me. I can't let the poison kill me, sibling, my work is too important. You were my *last* option, I promise you." I thought it was an accident that we collided earlier, but it was clearly by design. There's no way I would've been able to avoid touching a flower or grass blade that wasn't already contaminated and Weijia knew that. He must feel so powerless in the wake of the destruction—with all of his intellectual prowess, even *he* managed to be affected—and those consumed by their position of powerlessness are the first to desire power and dominion over the lives of others. I will gladly die knowing that I never became like the Titans—that I will never be a plague to life on this planet—even if I die by the actions of one who did. I will gladly die knowing that my prayer was answered, despite the fact that it was answered by a false deity. Amen.

INSIGHT: LOVE

We often lose sight of being present with those we care about, until we have to face the possibility of losing them.

– Another Way: Lachelle

I tell her that I love her.
I use three small words
in an attempt to describe
something that's
inconceivably simpler,
more complex,
and as old as
humanity's very existence.

– Uneven 2

I was lifted up so high,
loved and accepted
so deeply,
that soon the same
characteristics which first
inspired admiration began
brewing animosity
like a distillery.

- Augmented: Submersion

I rather be excited
about who I'm with,
than sure about them.

- Uneven

I stay up for hours
daydreaming of the
waking dream I will
experience the following
night—of the fantastical
that will be adorned
without formality,
of the depths of affection
that will be explored,
excavated, shared, and
spent frivolously.

— Mirage

I look deep into his eyes
and smile at him with mine.
I can see everything
he's running from,
and I show him everything
he'll find once he
finally gets away.

– For Hire: Apprentice

He taught me that
someone could
love me so much,
that all their love did
was accentuate how
different we were.

- Uneven 2

The future and past
have lost all relevance,
I just want more
of right now.

– For Hire: Master

I feel fortunate to have
spent a fair amount of time
around toxic people,
because their true purpose
is to confirm the value
of those who
should be treasured.

— Uneven 2

I say what I'm feeling
the only way
I know how,
by offering the words
to her like a sacrifice
brought to a goddess
on the fingertips
of a king.

— Mirage

She lifts my chin up,
looks deep into
my eyes and smiles
at me with hers,
and for the first time
I see freedom.

— For Hire: Apprentice

I've seen too many
relationships that are
based on expectation
rather than appreciation,
on control rather
than consideration.
Where there's this constant
undercurrent between those
involved to endlessly
grapple for the upper hand.

— Uneven 2

Seeing the world
through their eyes
was like looking at
a prism refracting light;
their passion and
inquisitiveness like
experiencing a
rainbow personified.

— Broken Hands

The hands are
an extension
of the heart.

- For Hire: Master

Whether between family,
friends, or lovers,
if not vigilant,
we can make the simple
pleasure of mutually
enjoying and appreciating
one another
unimaginably complicated.

– Uneven 3

She looks up
into my eyes and
writes me a love letter
from another planet,
speaking a language
that laughs at words.

— Mirage

I've wondered if
I should hate people,
even though I know
that the thing
I hate about them
the most is
missing them.

— Broken Hands

When all control is
lost to another,
the eyes are no longer
solely a window
to the soul,
they are a ballet.

– For Hire: Master

My only wish was
for people to treat me
like I was dead,
while I was still alive
to appreciate it.

– Uneven 2

Every conversation you
have with someone is
potentially an opportunity
to learn something
about them that
no one else knows.

— Uneven 2

ANOTHER WAY: SPENCER

Supposedly I'm a "spider", but I try not to subscribe to labels, I'm just me. I'm just trying to figure it all out. My mother used to tell me that we're heroes, all of us, because of what we do. She would go on and on about how we effortlessly brought balance and beauty into the world like none other in existence—"You are judge, jury, and architect of the courthouse," she'd say.

None of us were taught how to weave, we just did it. When it was time we would begin without objection, and we would continue until we had built what was necessary. I remember my first web, I was *so hungry* and my mother hadn't fed me in almost two full moons, so there was no choice. She showed me a section of leaves that would work for me, and I got to work. I did what I needed to do, or I would've been dead—my mother would've watched me starve to death had I not succeeded. That's the way it is: weave the web, or dine with the dead. If we are meant to be who we are to become, we will undoubtedly find a way to do so.

I was taught that no other arachnid's world rivaled our own, and that we are nothing like the insects we hunted—we have purpose. Mother called our webs a "geometric miracle", and I can say with the utmost humility, they are truly nothing short of miraculous. I've seen Weavers put together webs that I would've never thought possible. Rows upon rows within columns connected from leaf—to branch—to tree trunk, like a sprawling safety net ready to catch a falling flying trapeze artist. That isn't what we do though, is it? We don't weave in order to save life, we weave in order to take it. The grand "purpose" my mother described to me doesn't seem so grand at all. Although, even I watch in near disbelief as others like myself design their delicate, and deadly instruments of survival, security, and murder—at the right angle, the strand of the initial cord is invisible, and the Weavers hang in midair as if they've defied the laws of nature entirely—lately even I've been filled with more questions than adoration. Do we do what we do because it comes naturally, or because we were trained to utilize only a specified set of our available abilities? What if the only reason that we follow a path is because we were never shown that any other existed?

I don't argue with the fact that all of us must find a way to eat and live, but is killing in order to do so truly the only method? I don't think that it is. I don't argue with the balance that must be maintained. As the old legends say, flies of all species would suffocate the world beneath a blanket of their buzzing wings if not for us. My mother is dead. She died from a parasite that infected her brain, grew into a larva, and then slowly ate her body—there was nothing left for me to ceremoniously bury at her funeral. I don't argue with that either. She captured and devoured more insects than either

her or myself could count, so although I'm sad that my mother is no longer here, she was a menace. As it has become accepted in our colony, one of those she consumed was my father. She wanted me to weave, and eat, and grow as much as I could as quickly as possible so that I wouldn't "end up like him." I suppose time will tell whether I do or don't. According to her, she would've died herself had she not eaten him, but as far as I've been informed, she's the only one —*was* the only one—who knows if that's true or not. I've often been told that I look like her, which I obviously cannot change, but I refuse to act like her. I refuse to be a slave to the narrow-minded tendencies she instilled in me. I refuse to be a murderer.

I've been on a diet of plant nectar and pollen for about seven full moons now, and it's been liberating, but many do not agree with me. For some reason the more that Weavers heard of my decision to try another lifestyle, the more discussions developed to paint my perspective as unhealthy, and even destructive. I've been publicly accused of going against the natural order of life, and attempting to manipulate others into living as I currently am, so I fear that I may need to leave the colony soon. When there is no room to be different there is no room for freedom, and if I am forced to choose, I will choose freedom every time.

I've been weaving now only so that I can catch pollen, so my webs are smaller and I try to keep them out of the way of where insects frequently travel. According to the few friends that I have left, there are others who feel as I do but who fear pursuing an alternate avenue as I have after seeing how I've been mistreated. My plan is to stay here in the colony for as long as it's safe for me. I want to meet and help those who are interested in the possibilities. I want to show them that there *is* another way. My mother believed we're heroes, and I believe that maybe one day we could be just that.

ANOTHER WAY: JEROME

T he bees, they're the perfect example. We all know that every living organism has a job to do, and that every job is important, but we all know what it is that the bees do: they're the ones keeping us all alive. So, what if you have a bee who no longer wants to do his work as a bee? And that one bee then tells another bee, and the bee that he tells thinks his idea is pretty good, so now two bees aren't doing their work. Then those two bees tell two other bees, and as quickly as the suggestion was made and then adhered to, all of the vegetation on the planet is dead because the bees didn't want to be bees anymore. This is how the world works: everything can't be optional or redefined. Life is a test, every question is multiple-choice, and we all have two options: do what we're supposed to do in order to keep the world turning, or destroy everything due to a combination of misplaced self-righteousness and delusions of grandeur. There are no *new paths* to be etched into the soil of the Earth, only the ones that we're born into. There are no Authorists[7], only those who think they are; only those who

---

[7] Authorist Futurism: An Authorist acknowledges that the only thing ahead of them is a blank canvas. They believe the composition to fill that canvas is decided by nothing short of what they want for themselves, their will and determination to create it, and their readiness to see that what they intended may have taken on a different form, and presented a progressive opportunity that they could not have previously foreseen. Authorist Futurism encapsulates vision, action, and fluidity.

are seeing what was never there to begin with, and what will never be there regardless of how long they look for it.

This is what I'm dealing with at this very moment: a spider, scurrying about like a scared centipede, genuinely convincing other spiders that if they run off and do whatever they want, that they will miraculously be making the world a better place. It doesn't make any sense. I don't know what he tells them, but, like a parasite, he's clearly skilled at getting inside an individual's head. Myself and the other Peace Officers of the colony have been able to keep him from physically returning and spreading his message of anarchy, but from what we've seen, there are still members of his cult living among us who are secretly attempting to lead others astray. I've personally recovered pamphlets in the possession of suspected cult members describing our treasured traditions, passed down to us by our ancestors, as murderous and barbaric. The rhetoric urges the reader to not only turn their backs on the colony and all we stand for, but to also bring as many with them as they can. It's unfortunate the way in which ideas can become poison, and how we can infect one another with the disease of self-destructive perspectives. Those perspectives grow legs, and eyes, and ears, and mouths, and become living, breathing beliefs, and those beliefs—regardless of their validity—are what we live, kill, and die for. There are few things more fatal to who one is than being misunderstood, and few things more fatal to a collective than misinformation. This is what has kept myself and the others vigilant around the sun and moon—and even squinting while on guard under only the dim, distant light from the stars—in order to erase this dissension and restore order. During the last three cycles from dark sky to full moon, in our colony of just over 8,000, we've captured and convicted 63 conspirators, and estimated that a little over 100 of our own have deserted us. Those who have left and those who have stayed both know one thing: there is strength in numbers. And I, for one, would not be able to knowingly march to my death just to prove a point that will ultimately change nothing.

Tonight is one of my few nights off but I'm still listening to the scanners, and there was apparently a small caravan reported exiting the community. We didn't have people on the ground in that specific area, so they were gone by the time we got there. We'll have scouts out in the morning—I might go along as well—to hopefully find them and inform them of why this is a mistake that they may or may not survive long enough to regret. Still, our main efforts are focused here, in the colony, to prevent more poor decisions from being actualized. Based on our intel, the ones choosing to leave are our youngest adults—those who have just reached maturity, have only surpassed maturity for a short time, and some who are not even officially of age— and naturally, this hurts the most. We all hope that our actions, words, and wisdom can be used to assist with the progressive growth of those closest to us, but the reality is that our experiences can only guide those who truly seek guidance. Many would rather do what they want rather than what's best.

When I'm on patrol and discussing the recent events with those who have far surpassed their younger days, I can visibly see their demeanor change. Although subtle, it's clear they feel the same as I: that, due to the circumstances, we've managed to fail those who follow behind us. What I remind them of is this: that we are Weavers, maintainers of balance, and that this fight to hold our colony together—along with each individual in it—is nowhere near the end. I remind them of what has stood true for generations, that we only grow stronger from our struggle. I know that I will not quit, and that those on my team feel the same, so I'm confident we'll have this nonsense behind us soon. It's still painfully hard to believe that all of this chaos and unrest was caused by my only surviving brother, Spencer.

ANOTHER WAY: LACHELLE

No one can know that Spencer's dead. We've come too far and changed too much for the better to allow the sad, untimely demise of such a revolutionary figure derail the progress that he inspired. That's why as soon as the last ember went out from the fire that lifted his remains toward the heavens, I stepped in to do everything that he would have as if he'd never left us. If history has taught me anything—well, history has obviously taught me a *wealth* of things—it's that time and time again great movements have been turned into half remembered maxims once those who start the movement have fallen. No one expected this to happen when it did. No one except for me.

"Lachelle, can I speak with you? It won't take long."

"Of course, Spencer. Uma, can you take over, please? I'll be back soon."

"Perfect—walk with me. And thank you so much, Uma." Spencer always made it a point to remind us that neither himself, nor anyone else, was more important or held any higher status than any other—there were only equals here.

Naturally, we applied this ideal to our working environment, but he, as always, was thinking globally. He had a vision of a world that was soaked with the pursuit of equality and understanding of all life, where normalcy had no strict definition, and the only status quo was none at all. The goal of *Another Way* was simply to lead others to lead themselves, to broaden minds that were born into narrow corridors, to ignite intrigue and inquiry into new thoughts and ideas—as well as those long forgotten—and to encourage tangible outward expression of that which flourished within.

During the first conversation Spencer and I had, I told him how I'd been searching for something like this for longer than I could remember. The whole time we spoke I thought I was talking too much, but he listened so quietly that I couldn't stop myself. I remember telling him how I've always felt like life resembled an iceberg: only a small portion was visible on the surface and that symbolized life's aesthetic aspects, but beneath the surface held the majority of what mattered—wisdom, understanding, depth, and clarity. The next day he created a visual of my concept: a single-lined, four-sided, diamond-shaped symbol showing the difference in significance between the tip of the iceberg on the surface, versus the majesty that lay beneath—it was beautiful.

"How are things going, Lachelle? How are you feeling?"

"Things are going well! Just yesterday we had five more from the colony come to join us, and we're receiving positive reports back from our contacts that are still inside. A few arrests, unfortunately, but spiders are taking notice—they're interested—your words are getting through, Spencer." He raises an eye at me. "*The* words are getting through."

"That is very good to hear. Attaching actions to our passions is paramount if we wish to see progress, and I see that we have been doing well in this area. But, how are *you* feeling?" I was hoping that he wouldn't notice my blatant disregard of his second question, but, I knew that was a long shot.

"Well...there's been a few more than just a *few* arrests, and that's, of course, disheartening. The Peace Officers are pressing citizens for information and dragging them away whenever they can. If *you* could go into the colony to speak or encourage them, I think it would help greatly, but obviously you can't. You do have that effect though. Spiders trust what you have to say, and they value your perspective and energy."

"And that is the problem." I've never heard so few words delivered with such finality—like a priest reading a prisoner their last rites prior to their execution. I stopped walking and just looked at him, perplexed.

"Spencer, what does that mean exactly?"

He proceeded to detail what he'd observed, and how the movement was too dependent upon his presence. Additionally, he was concerned with the actions that were being carried out by the more militant supporters—actions that were not in-line whatsoever with what Another Way represented—and the fact that they were being carried out in his name. A fire was deliberately set at one of the food storage depots two Sun movements ago—a lot was lost—and in front of the freshly charred section of the colony, a sign was left that plainly stated "ALL HAIL SPENCER! FOLLOW ANOTHER WAY!" As one of the leaders of our communications team, Spencer modestly suggested to me that I get a message out to those we had on the ground to clarify that we didn't have, and will never have, any association with destructive action towards any part of the colony. The Peace Officers, and the media that propagate for them, of course, used this latest senseless attack to further vilify what it was that we stood for. Spencer saw everything as he always did, as a part of The Catalytic Principle—that of which, he was a firm believer. The principle stated that neither right nor wrong exist, there are only catalysts and non-catalysts. Either a person, action, or situation causes change, or it does not. Whether the catalysts are viewed as positive or negative is a perspective of one's own invention to more easily compartmentalize the way in which they are affected. And with all that was happening, he felt that there needed to be another catalyst introduced if things were going to continue progressively.

"I am going to kill myself, Lachelle."

"That's not funny."

"I'm not joking."

"Well, then you should *start*."

"You know that we can't stop our brothers and sisters from radicalizing themselves. Even when we say we don't support them, they think it's the Peace Officers attempting to deceive them. And, as you alluded to, if I personally enter the colony, there will be no escape for me."

"Then go into hiding!"

"You want me to live my life looking over my shoulder until I die, hoping that no one stumbles upon my whereabouts?"

"Isn't that better than being dead?!"

"Do you know something I don't?" At times he was incredibly unaffected, it was a mood he would get in, and it was as impressive as it was irritating.

"Fine, then we'll have the radicals come here to talk."

"And you think they won't be followed? You think the same group that's burning the colony's food and putting lives at risk isn't under more surveillance than even we are?" Naturally, he was right. Even as we spoke, there was only a slim chance that anyone suspected of having even an inkling of information, or relation to the radicals, wasn't already in custody. Spencer looked into my eyes and smiled at me with his, "This will move everything forward as it should be, I promise. Let everyone know that I'm gone, and you, along with everyone else will see how much my departure brings peace and further progress." We often lose sight of being present with those we care about, until we have to face the possibility of losing them. I wanted to stretch this moment out for as long as I could, because I knew that there wouldn't be any more with him in it.

Myself, Uma, and Jason found Spencer dead the next morning—we're the only three who know. We agreed that we'll let the world know when it's time to, and that now is not the time. That was nine full moons ago.

All hail, Spencer.

MIRAGE

S he looks up into my eyes and writes me a love letter from another planet, speaking a language that laughs at words and feels the same way that waves crashing against the sand sound—ancient, deep, and rhythmic. She's a lullaby that awakens rather than puts to rest. The letter is signed with three syllables that I can see like shooting stars on this dark, Spring night: "I love you"—and I believe every movement and vibration that send the sounds to my ears. I'm holding the universe so close that I can rest my chin on her shoulder, and suddenly I know what it must feel like to be God: to have everything imaginable, and unimagined, in your reach all at once.

Can she feel what I'm thinking? Does she already know that I can see through her, that she can finally stop pretending like she isn't who she is? Does she know that she's found home, the place she has drifted through time and space to find? The place her heart has never seen but has been impatiently waiting for? "I love you." I say it softly so only she can hear it, as if we're surrounded by onlookers and eavesdroppers trying to discover the secret to our magic. Inside me there's a choir singing of my love for her, with harmonies cascading like waterfalls into melodious rivers as wide, and as still, as forever. I say what I'm feeling the only way I know how, by offering the words to her like a sacrifice brought to a goddess on the fingertips of a king—I pray my incantation will bind her in human form for a few minutes longer. If only I could kiss her, then I could tell if I was successful. If only I could melt this moment of beautifully looped time that I'm frozen in—smiling when she smiles, laughing when she laughs. Without moving from where we stand, we manage to swirl around each other like snowflakes falling for eternity—falling, but never to reach the ground.

The quiet street light behind her powders her silhouette with a soft incandescence, and I carefully trace her outline in a single glance: she is the shape of happiness. She instinctively floats away from me so I can see more of her— gaze upon her—My Love, my weightless raindrop of simplicity within the ever-churning oceans of convolution. When I reach for her, like an illusionist, she instantly appears by my side once again. The magnetic energy that courses through us both, pulling one another near, is more alive than both of us combined.

Her eyes find mine like they are all she's been missing, as she stands close enough that her eyes are all I can see. On this lazily lit street, those eyes are a glimpse into two tarpits of the endless unknown, and I am caught, and I've surrendered, and I will sink deeper into them with elation.

What she would like to know is if we will see each other again, specifically, if we could see each other tomorrow night. The question is the "p.s." at the end of the letter she's already penned to me; an invitation to make the planets align instead of merely watching them do so. It's like Time asking me if she can add more sand to my hourglass, and if I would like her to slow the descent of each individual grain. If she suspects that my answer will be yes, she shows no sign of it. There's only a split second that passes before I accept the invite, but in that short time, Time drags it's feet, and My Love awaits my reply without expectation, but with a fire of burning excitement that radiates in every direction. I can feel it, so I release my response before we are both engulfed by the blaze. I stay up for hours daydreaming of the waking dream I will experience the following night—of the fantastical that will be adorned without formality, of the depths of affection that will be explored, excavated, shared, and spent frivolously. Still, I reminisce about the alluring words whispered between her and I under the cover of darkness, witnessed by a jury composed of stars, and a judge that sat as high as the moon. Anticipation, you are one of my most favored companions.

I never saw her again. There is no poetry here. I inquired if she was ready and she never responded. I asked if everything was alright, and she never responded. The same pattern continued with similar questions as the initial two—I never heard from her again. All of the excitement, and sincerity, and love, and want, that she displayed almost exactly 24 hours prior, meant nothing, or, only meant something at the time. There is, of course, *The Principle of Emotional Truth* to be considered, and that's different than the truth some believe to be absolute. Emotional Truth is always changing, as is characteristic of emotions themselves. Emotional Truth is that which is true only in the moment that it's experienced. The words are felt to be true when they are said, the actions are felt to be true when they are performed, and the thoughts are felt to be true when they are thought of, but prior to that moment, they didn't exist and after that moment, they are lifeless until brought back to life once more. Lifeless, as lifeless as she is to me and I to her, like all life: here in an instant, and gone instantaneously. How unfortunate it is that we don't wholly control with whom we fall in love, and that I am once again alone. How unfortunate it is that I fell in love with a ghost.

BROKEN HANDS

My phone chimes at me that I have a new text message, and when I look at the screen I see this: "Is the loneliness getting to you, or is it the realization that you're alone?" I read the message twice, and then place my phone face down and pretend like I didn't read it at all. It was too early in the morning to answer questions that force me to question my existence, and frankly, it wasn't a fair question to ask in the first place.

I'm too old to be playing this game. I'm too old to be worried about the past, and who said what to whom—do you know what the past is good for? Reminding you of everything you'll never be able to change because it's already happened, and once it's happened, that's it—no going back. Do you know what else the past is good for? Reminding you of everything you had that you've lost. You remember what you lost, how you lost it, and how you tried to get back but never could. So, every day since then you've been senselessly chasing a cheetah on foot, trying to recapture a time that's barely a blurred image seen from the corner of your eye, yet —irrationally—it still remains the most clearly beautiful moment that you can recall, even though in reality it wasn't. That's how the past juggles with your sanity: it makes the piranhas look like puppies. The connection may not be clear to you currently, but the connection is there nevertheless, like the Sun when the weather's overcast—it illuminates half of a planet, while being able to hide behind pockets of water vapor that barely measure a recordable fraction of it's size. The connection is that the past *is* the path that got me here— the same path that got you here, and got everyone else here —so if you ask anyone a question about how they feel in this exact instance, what you're really asking them about is their past, and how they arrived at their present location. Don't be surprised if they have a good reason to refrain from divulging every detail or don't see the point of discussing any of it at all. Maybe they value their time. Maybe they're like me and they've realized what I've realized: that those around me don't understand the world as I do, so I must understand the world as they do—*Stabilizing Assimilation Law*. It's not an observation regarding "blending in" socially or culturally, but the unconsciously or consciously objective recognition of a personal disconnect regarding what is viewed to be acceptable of ones species on the most elementary of psychological levels, and the understanding that for the maintenance of daily mental stability, one must retain a level of adherence to that which has been generally accepted as natural. In other words, if they're like me, they will always question every action, thought, and inclination regarding what it means to be alive, or dead, or human, or non-human. They will accept nothing as simply being the way that it is— not even aspects of themselves—but they will see that in order to make it through each day, it's necessary to see existence as others do who, for whatever reason, see less to question, or nothing to question at all. Maybe these outcasts and outsiders will never be able to play the part convincingly enough. They'll never be able to tell the girl exactly what she wants to hear, or pretend that guy is as smart as he thinks he is, or answer the questions in ways that will lead to no further questions being asked. Maybe they're not like everyone else, maybe assimilating rings like an unanswered rotary telephone every time they get anywhere close to it. Maybe people don't understand why their mask just can't seem to stay on long enough for them to join the masquerade quietly. Maybe they're not fake enough to be another plastic soldier melted under a 93°F sun into a withered, twisted, and half disfigured version of themselves by a child given nothing better to do than hold a magnifying glass in their direction at exactly the correct angle—maybe they're not meant to die.

I happen to love being immortal, I love knowing this never ends for me, and that I have more time than I'll ever need to do everything I can imagine. Sleeping becomes difficult, but in a theoretical sense—at least for me—because I wouldn't sleep through the night even if I could. I wouldn't want to miss any of the show because I love the spectacle of the carousel ride far too deeply. Round and round it turns, the lights pulsating rhythmically as a visual heartbeat of the music being played—a soundtrack to translate the emotion of every passing second. The children shout with excitement, laugh overjoyed, or hold on for dear life unable to overcome their apprehension; others hop off of their mechanical horses and explore the carousel on foot even while it spins—this is the human experience. Unless you're looking for, or creating a dull moment, you'll go blind attempting to find one. Then there's the planet itself that never rests. Even when the people have long since surrendered to the inevitability of their beds, and their eyes sink low as if an anchor has dragged them to the depths of the sea, that only lets loose the broader, more subtle expressions which then step forward to occupy center stage. The full moon shines like a spotlight—using its borrowed glow from the sun, which stands unseen behind the curtain—to softly accentuate all that lays beneath it. If fortune has found it fit to smile upon you, the crickets are now in control of the sounds and play a soft, trance-inducing lullaby left on repeat. The earthy melody has no choice but to remind you to live here—right now—because right now is the only thing you have that's promised, and in it's promise lies the one and only appearance of perfection. I wouldn't want to waste time laying around with my eyes closed and my ears muted, now would I? That doesn't sound engaging in the slightest.

Naturally, as it is with all that exists, there is a less desirable aspect to living forever as well. If I'm being honest there many aspects, but I rather not purposefully fill my mind with all that exhausts it. When, or if, I decide to answer the message I was sent today, the answer to the question regarding loneliness will be this: it is the realization of how alone one truly is that reaches the greatest depths. And in this existence, nothing that can be experienced affects one more than the depth at which the experience is felt. The scale, duration, frequency, aesthetic, utility, and worth—for example—may all intersect at one point or another, but it is depth that will leave the most lasting impression.

As you can imagine, it becomes challenging to keep people around when you're the one outliving them. When you realize that no matter how much you care about people, and love them, and appreciate them, and strive to make them happy, that in the end it doesn't matter. In the end, you'll lose them and you'll never get them back, because they're gone, and you're still here, still alive, without them. The more you try to get them back, the wider the chasm between you grows, until you wonder if you only imagined yourself in the company of others that cared about you to begin with. You wonder if there was ever a time that you weren't the only one left at the table, eating dessert, after everyone else had gotten their check and left because they had already had enough. I've wondered if there was ever a time that I wasn't alone—if I'm repeating myself I don't care, this is important—I've wondered if I should hate people, even though I know that the thing I hate about them the most is missing them. I've thought about killing myself, but I'd have to hire someone to do it for me. Death would erase the memory of those I've lost, and killing the memory would be killing all that I have left of them. Killing the memory would be like bringing death to my loved ones once more, and that, that I could never bring myself to do. I am not a murderer.

The one who inspired my current path was my unforgettably captivating ninth love—they were everything. Every time I heard their voice I fell in love with them again, and again, but they weren't mine, and said they never truly could be—although they shared my feelings. They were like me, immortal, but they were exhausted; they'd already had their fill of living lifetime after lifetime, and they just couldn't consume any more.

We were married a million times, in a million beautiful times, and still none were as breathtaking as they were. I admired them like a discovery, like an unearthed gem that held the power to unearth me. Seeing the world through their eyes was like looking at a prism refracting light; their passion and inquisitiveness like experiencing a rainbow personified. How many lifetimes had we been everything to each other; been exactly what we longed for, needed, and wanted? More times than can be remembered; more times than should even be possible—it was evident in every interaction we had. True love is timeless, and true love has a name, and it was Us.

I knew everything they loved, and I gave it to them as if I always had a surplus, even when I didn't. I was their own personal psychic, I knew what they wanted before they did, and made sure they had it before they even had to ask. It was my pleasure to do so, and they treated me likewise. I never felt more understood and appreciated, even when we had the knives out with the business end at each other's throats, there wasn't anyone else I'd want as my adversary. We could make each other feel less than human all day, and more than human all night; we were black magic practitioners, and every word we uttered—or didn't—was a spell that interlaced us closer together. Their was no other face I wanted to see more, no opinion I placed a higher value on, none who so effortlessly reminded me of who I was when I could barely recognize the back of my own hand—but they had unquestionably had enough, of all of it. When they expressed to me that they would not only be voluntarily departing from my side, but from existence itself, I became the ocean, and I wept until the seas became dry land. They would never wholly be mine, nor I their's, because this life was, at once, too much for them and also not enough. Another connection severed. Another instance of my mind left scrambling to decipher, and comprehend the code of free will and perception, where no code existed.

The question then arises: is loss, at it's core, about who or what is lost, or is there something else? My story is hardly one of a relationship turned cold. What I lost was a bond, something to tether me to the maze of reality I wandered through; I lost the constellations in the night sky that confirmed my location in the universe. The mind will use all that it has at it's disposal to rectify that which defies personal logic; it will create as many narratives as needed, at whatever depth is mandated, in order for one to make sense of what has been taken from them—my mind did the same. It's the loss of that bond to reality that drives one to the cliffside of madness, and parks the car with half of it hanging over the edge; the loss of a tangible place in existence—of a language spoken by the chaos—expressing that "You are recognized; you have a home." When I lost them, my mirror, the rest of my surroundings cracked, and shattered along with it. It wasn't the absence of their love or companionship that broke me, but the absence of what they represented.

The realization that I'm alone shouldn't shock me after all these years. By this time, it should merely be another breath taken, another blink of an eye, another beat of my heart. It should be no less a part of me than any of the forgotten, or never noticed bodily functions, that mentally and physically allow me to continue living in the manner to which I've grown addictively accustomed. But on a day like today, when

I'm directly questioned about my life, the depths at which this desolate reality reside are awakened and rise like a tsunami to overtake me, and I'm shocked once again. Haunted by seclusion that violently engrosses my every thought; formless apparitions howl with echoing shrieks of silence...with echoing shrieks of silence...with echoing shrieks of...

Everything is borrowed, everything except the desertion. New ones arrive but they don't understand you, they only say they do. They don't want to know the crevices of who you are, they only say they do. They don't see the world the way that you see it—how could they? They only say they do. They don't relate to your experiences or want to be there by your side when you've lost yourself, they only say they do. And their words mean nothing because their words are just as lonely as you are. Then they leave, just like everyone else. If you're like me, then I've faced what you've faced, I've only faced it for longer. I've chosen to live alone for eternity rather than die alone and have to face my greatest fear. What remains faithful to us all is *The General Ownership Phenomenon:* we are born into a world grounded in the illusionary ideal of possession. From the items we purchase, create, and collect, to the people we befriend, give birth to, and love, to the bodies we inhabit and utilize to experience internal and external stimuli (the creation and capture of memories), it's only a matter of time or circumstance before all is proven impermanent. The illusion of ownership is then revealed to be the most feeble and ultimately destructive device used by humanity to validate their existence, because the promise and expectation of permanence will either be revealed as deception or failure. The volatility of our environment may seem like another bitter, unsightly facet of life, but in actuality, it's the reason why life is worth living; presenting us with a dazzling opportunity: to be in a state of constant wonder and gratitude. We own nothing, we keep nothing, therefore we lose nothing—we are free. Everything is borrowed. Everything is borrowed except the desertion. This is the phenomenon that too many of us are hanging onto; some holding on by hand, others by their neck.

All of this I know definitively to the degree that I would question the blood flowing through my veins before I question this principle that, without exception, has humbly stretched across the expanse of generations. Yet, here I am, privileged to live as an Existant[8]. I'm privileged to live as a creation creating, as an expression expressing, as an experience experiencing, while plagued by the inescapable, cyclical nature of time: birth, death, and rebirth; find, return, then find again. All of this I know, yet the realization brings storm-clouds to my soul and rain drops to my eyes all the same. I have no choice but to wait for this period of isolation to subside, and request of the powers that be that my patience is rewarded with anything other than disappointment. Thankfully, I *do* have the choice of where my focus is placed: either on my immediate environment, which finds me wading through neck-high, leech-filled waters, or, on my Earthly environment, which creates beauty and life on a magnitude that defies even immortality. I would like to choose the latter, but time will tell.

---

[8] One with the following characteristics: consciousness (the awareness of internal and external existence), self-awareness (the recognition of consciousness and the capacity for introspection), sentience (the ability to feel pain and pleasure), sapience (the ability to think and act utilizing wisdom and insight); a combination of the words *existing* + *internally* (creating the term *Existant*), since the essence of who one is lives within; not characteristics that are exclusive to Homo Sapiens.

I pick up my phone, reopen the message, and silently read it to myself once more: "Is the loneliness getting to you, or is it the realization that you're alone?"—I'm ready to respond now: "all of the above."

INSIGHT: MOTIVATION

If we're meant
to be who
we will become,
we will undoubtedly
find a way to do so.

- Another Way: Spencer

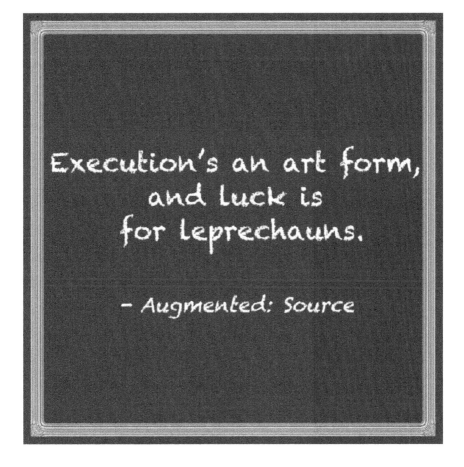

Execution's an art form,
and luck is
for leprechauns.

— Augmented: Source

Attaching actions to
our passions is
paramount if we
wish to see progress.

– Another Way: Lachelle

No one knows if what
they consider to be the
worst possible outcome
will end up being
the precise catalyst
they need the most.

— The Undead Eye: Will

I'll always ask
the obvious questions,
because I know
the answers are
seldom obvious.

– Uneven 3

All he knows is that he'll die trying to change the world before it changes him.

— Darker Vision

We only grow
stronger from
our struggle.

- Another Way: Jerome

Lead others
to
lead themselves.

– Another Way: Lachelle

A part of him
knew that creating an
image of success,
based on the failures or
successes of others,
produced
warped expectations.

- Uneven

I didn't want to lose
the familiarity of tradition,
nor the ease of the habitual.
It's tradition and habit
that form so much of
the ground we stand on,
but once they're removed,
standing is no longer an
option—we must learn to fly.

— Beware

What if the only reason
we follow a path
is because we were
never shown that
any other existed?

– Another Way: Spencer

There were always
going to be situations
that would make me
question my validity,
but they were only questions,
ones that I had to
ceaselessly answer with the
handwritten sheet music to
the song of my identity.

- Uneven 2

Anywhere can feel
like home if you
want it to be.

- The Undead Eye: Kennedy

When my back is
against the wall,
at least I know that
everything I need to
face is right in
front of me.

– The Undead Eye: Will

We're all alive to
reconnect with ourselves,
all alive to
be who we are.

– Augmented: Submersion

When there's no room
to be different
there's no room
for freedom.

- Another Way: Spencer

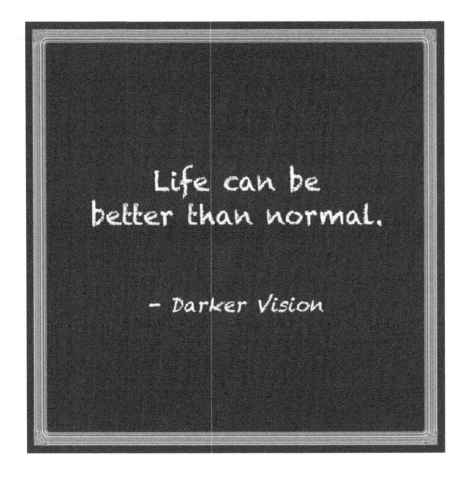

Life can be
better than normal.

- Darker Vision

I've always known that progress requires sacrifice, and that most aren't willing to lose what brings them comfort in order to gain what's necessary for success.

— The Undead Eye: Dr. Gren

Right now is the
only thing you
have that's promised,
and in it's promise lies
the one and only
appearance of perfection.

- Broken Hands

You can't discover
anything new
under the sun,
if you're afraid
to stare into it.

— Augmented: Source

UNEVEN

Damien Jeffries walked with a limp that he could've easily had fixed years ago, but he chose not to—the awkward stride was a part of him now. He'd rather keep the pain as a reminder of what he'd survived, and also as a daily obstacle that he had to overcome every time he took a step. The pain was indicative of his strength, and he never wanted that taken away from him. He'd walk with a limp for the rest of his life if it reminded him of how strong he was, and he's not the only one. How many purposefully place themselves in difficult situations and never really try to fix them because if they did, they'd have nothing left to remind them of who they are? To some, their resilience defines their identity to such a large degree that without having a constant external struggle, they struggle to find an avenue for their energy. Without the obstacles, Jeffries was a vampire staring into a mirror, robbed of his own reflection. Coincidentally, he was actually quite fond of mirrors because he wasn't a vampire at all, he was a *Gezien*: someone who can make themselves invisible—a classification he had no knowledge of prior to learning what he was. At times, the only thing that could ground him was finding a mirror and staring deep into his own eyes. It was the closest thing to seeing who he was on the other side of the skin and bones he found so trivial. We've all heard that what matters about someone is who they are on the inside, but Jeffries lived that fact to an extent many wouldn't be able to comprehend. He knew without a doubt that no one's body embodies who they are, and that what is most real in this world will always elude the naked eye.

Prior to his injury, his life was essentially unblemished. At the age of nine he discovered his extraordinary abilities while running away from a neighborhood dog that had gotten loose. He was panicked, as he had never been chased by a dog before, and he truthfully thought his life was at risk and he needed to disappear. His body delivered in a way that he didn't know was possible. Naturally, the discovery confused and frightened him, but after overcoming the initial shock, all he had to do was get out of sight temporarily and he could then completely vanish at will. Most people live their entire lives doing only what they're supposed to, but Jeffries had been gifted with a truly unequaled opportunity that he initially used in one of the most immature ways possible: theft.

He might as well have ridden a magic carpet through school. He was his own personal genie, and whenever he needed to ace a test, poof, he'd magically have the answer key and didn't even have to rub a magic lamp. Periodically, he'd even get a B so his grades weren't too excessive, just over-achieving enough that he'd never get asked if he did his homework. From middle school, all the way through four years of college partying like a Greco-Roman emperor, life was pretty simple. As he grew older, like a suitcase handcuffed to his wrist, he carried around an exaggerated smirk that seldom left his face—most of the time he didn't even know it was there. Years went by where he was the last one to enter behind closed doors, the first set of eyes on messages that no one else should've seen, the interpreter of whispered conversations, and the lone witness to what most would consider to be the truth. This was why, even if he wanted to, he couldn't erase the smirk. He saw through people firsthand as they masqueraded in their carefully crafted costumes, and he found it absolutely hilarious. What he learned about the truth many wouldn't be interested in: that the truth isn't owed to anyone, that the truth is a luxury item everyone owns, but that isn't freely given away—if ever. Jeffries sat courtside and watched as people played the game. Back and forth they ran, either defending what they wanted to keep hidden, or going on the offensive to push what they wanted others to believe. He found that the truth is often requested, but what's truly desired is something that one already agrees with. Everyone was lying, either to themselves or others, and Jeffries found it perpetually funny; funny *and* sad, but he'd rather laugh than cry.

At the age of 27, he was a private investigator being paid generously to stand in the corner of ballrooms under $10,000 chandeliers that sparkled like sunlight on the ocean. Meanwhile, he contemplated the baffling paradox of how there were actually people who believed that having money and having taste were biologically related, and how he was surrounded by these people from wall to wall. During this same time in his life he was—again, being paid generously— traveling to off-coast islands whose names he couldn't pronounce, that were half untouched jungle, half tourist trap. There he'd spend maybe 30 hours in a quasi-war zone, and five days in a beach chair with his feet in the sand. Damien Jeffries knew that the only thing worse than being invisible was being dispensable, so he made himself the exact opposite. For the people that didn't want anyone to know that they were looking for information, he was a gatherer of information that no one else could seem to collect. Private investigating came naturally to him—for obvious reasons, and other reasons that were not so obvious—and because he was a Gezien, he occupied a class exclusive to himself. Life was graciously giving him more than he could ever ask for. Yet, naturally, there was a downside: when one is extremely good at something, it's difficult to keep it a secret for very long, and even more difficult to keep people from fervently wanting to know what your secret *is*.

It was Jeffries' left leg that he couldn't put pressure on, so even when he was standing still his body would lean to the right. Before the injury, his sister would always make fun of him for standing up too straight. She once messaged him a picture of an obelisk in Egypt with the caption "Look at u in Egypt without me. No invite??" He responded with a romantically-lit, perfectly-blurred background photograph of nothing but his middle finger. His sister, Anasia, found this particularly amusing—he loved their relationship. At any given time, he would easily consider his sister to not only be his cherished sibling, but his best friend as well. Still, Jeffries didn't even let *her know* what he was, as to not burden her with the knowledge—she had enough to worry about.

Anasia was lesbian, and when she came out to their parents, they disowned her; not right away, but after thinking about it they just decided that this person they created wasn't created by them anymore. That was it. It's as if no matter how far along society progresses, there will always be a status quo, and those who live and act outside of it are an inexplicable threat merely by living their lives. "Once all of that happened, it was just me and her. She's so strong, and smart, and inquisitive. She didn't deserve that, she didn't deserve to be made the enemy, and she doesn't ever deserve that again. I tried talking to them—you know I did—but no matter how I phrased things, or what examples I used, there was nothing that they would listen to, that made sense to them, or could broaden their perspective. This is *their child* I was talking about! All they had to do was lie, one small lie to allow their daughter to go into the world feeling like her parents loved and accepted her. They should've just listened to me. They should've given her that much, that much they owed her. The whole world is making up the truth every minute by the minute, and they couldn't create one comforting fact for their own child to hold on to—just one— but you already knew that." This is how he spoke to his mirror. It was about seven inches long and had a fold out stand so he could sit his confidante wherever he wanted. There were two carry-on bags that he owned that were his favorites, and he had a mirror in each of them just to make sure he was never without one. There was no one else that he could trust with his ruminations, not now that he had lived the life he lived. No one was who they outwardly portrayed, and because of this simple and proven observation, he only confided in his mirrors. And Anasia.

Jeffries' sister was in her second year of college, so he tried not to be that big brother that was constantly checking up on his little sister, but surprisingly—and to his delight— she called or messaged him much more than he expected. At least three times a week they'd talk and update each other on either school or work, and share funny or dramatic stories that would've been too exhausting to type via text message.

"Okay, so, wait: *who said* Annette was fat?!"

"Oh my god, it was Jalise—*as always!*"

"Asia, get your girl, bruh."

She bursts out in laughter.

"I swear I'm trying!"

When they weren't talking on the phone, they would still casually text short messages to one another with things that reminded them of times they shared in the past. Naturally, he was then concerned that she wasn't adjusting well, or didn't have *enough* friends, or was feeling homesick—he worried about her the way he wished someone would worry about him. Still, her grades were solid (mostly B's and a few A's) and based on her social media posts, she seemed to have a fairly healthy social life, but of course he knew how misleading appearances could be. Like all good guardians, he never really stopped worrying about her, he just tried to trust that if she needed anything she'd tell him. Motivation wasn't something that he had to worry about. The money that he made from his private investigating work is what paid for his sister's education and there was no way that he would fail her the way that their parents did. There was a part of him that knew creating an image of success, based on the failures or successes of others, produced warped expectations, but when it came to his little sister—his only loved one—he would be whatever she needed him to be.

During Anasia's fourth year of school the calls and texts diminished. She had a serious girlfriend now that Jeffries had already heard about through a plethora of texts and hours of conversation. He would've loved to keep up with their communication, but she was happy and he knew that, and he understood—at least one of them should have a little romance in their life. They'd known each other for over a year, and Jamie, Anasia's girlfriend, seemed to be a great fit for her. She was very supportive and helped Anasia land a difficult editing internship through some friends she had, so he truly couldn't be happier for his little sister. Being a good big brother, he did mention to her that he could look into Jamie's background just to be sure that nothing came up—that she wasn't hiding anything—but of course, Anasia refused.

"I know you're my genius brother that knows everything, but—"

"Wait, I *never* said that I know everything."

"Sure, whatever—but you don't need to know everything about something to know that it's good for you."

"So you don't want to be sure about who you're dealing with?

Anasia stopped and thought about this for a moment.

"No. I rather be excited about who I'm with than sure about them."

Jeffries and his sister didn't agree on this topic whatsoever, and since he hadn't met Jamie yet he hadn't had the chance to observe her. Even without his abilities as a Gezien, he could find out more than enough by patiently watching, listening, and engaging—people tell you who they are without saying a word and he knew that. Sure he could run around invisibly following people like a stalker, or he could pay attention and know when and where people would want to hide or discuss what he needed. But if his sister was comfortable living in the unknown, then he'd do his best to respect that. She had always been more on the side of following how she felt about people, not necessarily what she knew—the opposite of her brother. From his experience, people were like a full moon: they may feel or appear close to you, but in reality they're actually millions of miles away.

As it had been for years, Jeffries had his work to focus on, but business wasn't as lucrative as it had usually been. Although he wasn't getting contacted as much—now, at age 31—he rarely actually needed to work since he had plenty of money. He had his regulars, but other than that, he began to turn down more jobs than he was accepting. His clientele's attitude was shifting, and they were asking far more questions regarding the logistics of his methods. He couldn't match a name to the face, but something was different and it was right in front of him. Having made a career from personifying the idea that what's seen is only as important as what isn't, he'd be paying closer attention to anything that didn't attract any. Even his last job, three weeks ago in Venice, was strange enough to deserve a perplexed eyebrow raise.

Jeffries was requested to deliver his investigative findings in person, which was odd because usually no one wants the slightest possibility of being seen with, or even seen in the same vicinity as him. Jeffries loved Venice. The city was riddled with tall, stone buildings that created alleyways almost completely hidden from sunlight, even on the brightest days. At any given time it was like he was physically moving through one big, city-sized secret—he was in his element. It was in one of those particular alleyways where he was scheduled to meet his client and was told to knock four times on the door marked 14. He arrived invisibly, checked the area, materialized, and then knocked on the door, but there was no answer. After checking the time he was able to confirm what he already knew, that he was there exactly when he was supposed to be. He put his ear to the door but didn't hear any movement, and he tried opening it but it was locked. Luckily he still didn't see anyone else in the alley—no visible cameras either—but just in case, he took his phone out of his pocket, pretended to answer a call, and walked away speaking loudly. "I'm at 14 right now, where are you? *114?!* Are you—are you *serious?* Okay, okay, just gimme a minute. I'll be right there." When he did get in touch with his contact they actually said the same thing, that he was at the wrong door. The message sent to him had fallen victim to human error, as it should've said the door number *41* instead of 14. This was the second occurrence of nearly the exact same situation, and the double-vision was giving him a headache. A month prior to Venice, rearranged digits, another locked door, with a different client, but this time in Tijuana. He believed in coincidence about as much as he believed in the truth, and his suspicion was beginning to weigh on his mind like a tumor. Yet, with his sister thoroughly blossoming in her adulthood it left him with an unruly amount of time on his hands, so he figured why not get a few more jobs in, and then make some tangible plans regarding what he wanted the remainder of his life to look like. Who knows, maybe even lay low permanently.

His plane landed early to McCarran International Airport in Las Vegas, so when Jeffries got to his small, out-of-the-way hotel, he sat on his bed, put his feet up, and gave his sister a call. It'd been more than two weeks since they'd last spoke. Her phone rang, and rang, before it finally went to her voicemail, and he listened to her entire greeting just to hear her voice before hanging up. A text from her arrived a minute later letting him know that her and Jamie were in a movie, but that she'd call him as soon as they were out. Was he missing the joke? Doesn't she remember that she said the same thing only a few days ago? Even as an excuse, why not think of something else? Wow, just wow. The shock of what he was doing immediately hit him like accidentally biting the inside of his cheek. Anasia was the closest person to him in the entire world, and he basically raised her every chance that he could. She was his best friend and yet the thought actually crossed his mind to try to see through her—he felt like he was in a body-sized, burlap bag of embarrassment and shame. The job, having to hide away everything real about himself, the extreme psychological freedom *and* confinement of being a Gezien, even after all these years, was obviously getting to him because he wasn't thinking clearly. One can be so good at seeing what's out of place, that soon even that which is in its proper position can spark skepticism; the advantage and the affliction. Maybe the room was having an effect on him, it felt abnormally confining, like he was always about to walk into something. The way it was arranged was just odd: none of the furniture was aligned straight or flush against the wall, so it minimized the available space he had to move. A nap, that's what he needed, then he'd be fresh again—sharp—and he could fix the room later. Shirt off. Sweatpants on. Blinds closed. A little water to drink. Alarm set. Goodnight.

When his alarm went off and he habitually hit the snooze button, he knew it was time for work. No opportunity for erroneous thoughts or distractions. In 45 minutes, he needed to be on Las Vegas Boulevard, so he could vanish into an overpriced restaurant and begin his research on his latest subject. After getting dressed, in order to calm his mind he would sit silently either in a closet or the bathroom for exactly eight minutes and focus on one thought: noticing everything. The closet and bathroom resonated with him as isolated, so he went into one or the other to center himself. The closet didn't have enough room for him to fit comfortably, so he walked into the bathroom, didn't turn on the lights, closed the door, sat on the floor, set the timer on his phone for eight minutes, and closed his eyes. Sitting with his legs crossed Indian style, he rested his hands on his thighs, inhaled and exhaled deeply, then the most explosive pain he'd ever felt detonates in his left leg "Ahhh!" He yelled without restraint or composure. Reaching down, he felt a large hunting knife handle protruding out from just above his left knee. His heartbeat sounded like a paint bucket being played by a city street performer. This was impossible. Although he couldn't see anyone, he could feel that they were standing right in front of him, and he could hear their breath. But there was no way someone could've been hiding in this small bathroom. It was impossible.

"I didn't want it to be you, you should know that. I wanted it to be someone else—anyone else. This isn't what I ever wanted."

"Anasia?!"

"I'm sorry, Le'Andre. I'm sorry about all of this." She apologizes—calling her brother by his real name, Le'Andre— but it sounds nothing at all like an apology, more like the audible enunciation of his casket being closed, and lowered into a six-foot hole in the ground.

"Jesus Christ, Asia! How the—?! Okay, you know what? It's okay—I don't know what this is about or how this is even possible, but whatever you think that you want to do right now, we can talk about it. Let's just talk about it, okay? What is it? What do you need from me?"

If she responded to him, he couldn't hear it. His ears had broken into a piercing, uncontrollable ringing unlike anything he'd ever experienced. His whole body had turned into a distraught newborn screaming at the top of its lungs. The lights in the bathroom snapped on aggressively and forced his eyelids into a squint, but when he opened them, the bathroom was empty. And Anasia was there. But she also wasn't. Impossible, that's all he could think of, that one stupid word. No one could be there. Was he delusional? At some point had someone poisoned him? When's the last time he ate or drank anything? No one could *know* he was there, he was more than careful, more than cautious, but the more one tries to hide, the more they inevitably expose. No one was visibly in the bathroom with him, but he knew that he had just spoken to his sister, and he was sitting in pain that felt like every nerve in his body was pinched. None of this made sense, how could it? Panicked, he struggled to catch his breath, like he was his nine-year-old self being chased by that dog all over again. He'd never been stabbed before. He realized he'd never known what the word pain even meant prior to this moment. He didn't know if he should be worried about bleeding out or having a heart attack when finally, his little sister, Anasia, materialized right in front of him. The first thing he saw was her right hand stained red, and he couldn't take his eyes off of the proof of what his own sister had just done to him; it stared back at him seeming to wear the same smirk as he once did—how ironic.

Le'Andre Ruffin, code name Damien Jeffries, would never get his leg fixed because he always wanted to remember that day. He always wanted a physical reminder of everything that he already knew, and everything that had found a way to elude him.

UNEVEN 2

Ever since I can remember we all knew it, that something about my brother, Le'Andre, was different, only we didn't know what it was. He was special and I was just me. There wasn't even a sibling rivalry between us, whatever there was to win he had already won. Because of him, our parents were waiting for me like I was the mail carrier to deliver something—*anything*—that would incite the same feeling of otherness that he had. Eventually I did, but it wasn't the otherness that they were hoping for. There are only two ways to be unique: one way sparks intrigue, and the other sparks fear—coming out didn't spark any intrigue. While my brother became bust-worthy academic and social royalty without so much as wrinkling his t-shirt, I was regarded as a peasant and sat in shackles, watching through the iron bars of my cell in the dungeon, with nothing to do but wonder why I was there and how I could escape. Once the depression moved into the cell alongside me, I thought about killing myself. I thought about killing myself a lot actually, and the way in which my departure would be made. What would be best? I could do it where no one would find my body, or where I'd be the first thing people saw in the morning. There were pills, slitting my wrist, cutting my thigh, jumping off a bridge, whether to leave a note versus no note to leave people guessing why I did it—there's a lot to consider. My cousin killed herself when she was 22, and we were all deeply devastated. She was all our family talked about for months; her presence was longed for, her memory was priceless. We canonized her, and she became our own personal saint, even if she was never very saintly while she was with us. Through my sadness I envied her intensely. I craved what she didn't even know she had: the forgiveness, the adoration, the relentless outpouring of unconditional love, the treasuring of everything she was. It made me wonder if that's where the concept of heaven or paradise truly originated from, that "when I die is when I'll finally and wholly be appreciated, as well as shown the meaning of all that I struggled with, and struggled through." *My* only wish was for people to treat me like I was dead, while I was still alive to appreciate it. I know for a fact that my cousin, contrary to what she'd hoped, spent her 21st birthday alone, yet her funeral was standing room only. Meanwhile, my parents heard that I would be at the funeral, so they were one of the few that weren't in attendance. I heard that they went to the viewing, but apparently couldn't stand to be in the same room as me even to mourn a family member. If only they could treat me like I was my brother.

What made it worse was that my brother loved me, he may have loved me more than he loved himself and *he* was the one with that ineffable, magnetic personality. So as much as he loved me, as much as he tried to show me how cherished I was, he really only made things worse. It was he who taught me that, like all human action, love can be helpful as well as harmful. He taught me that someone could love me so much that all their love did was accentuate how different we were. I wanted to kill myself because my own brother made me feel like I didn't belong simply by being in my life. As soon as people knew we were related, they looked at me like a nightclub bouncer who couldn't find my name on the VIP guest list, and soon I began to view myself as they did. I thought that maybe I felt like I didn't belong here because I actually didn't, and if that was true, then why stick around at all? I was already alive and alone, so being dead and alone didn't sound any more painful. Assuming that I wouldn't know I was alone at all, it'd actually be a lot better. I couldn't be alone if I didn't know I was alone—or could I? In any case, I never ended up finding out. I didn't kill myself because I discovered that I was more than "just me", it turned out that I was more special than I ever could've imagined. I could make myself invisible, me, Anasia Ruffin. The girl who feared that she'd live her whole life being invisible, could *literally* be invisible whenever she wanted and do almost anything. I felt like the ink at the end of a poet's pen. There are few circumstances that breathe life into the inanimate like becoming one with that which they feared. Like one who has gone their entire life with a fear of snakes eventually being convinced to hold one, and realizing they're quite fond of the animal and its nature—a door to further discovery is instantly opened. This is why attaining knowledge of one's self has no equal. Mentally I was in a place where suicide didn't only seem like the easiest option, but also the most sensible, and I was in that place because I didn't know who I was. It wouldn't have mattered how well I was doing in school, how many friends I had, how much money I was making, or who cared about me. There were always going to be situations that would make me question my validity, but they were only questions, ones that I had to ceaselessly answer with the handwritten sheet music to the song of my identity. At its root, depression is a disease of ignorance, and there was no way I was returning to that place again; not for my parents or anyone else, not even for Le'Andre.

Initially I used my new found abilities in one of the most immature ways possible: theft. It was the summer before I started college when I realized what I was capable of, so when I got to campus I used my capabilities. I felt like I was owed that much. Since I wasn't ever that great at school, I thought it wise to only get grades that made it look like I was "getting it" a little more than I was before. I sprinkled in an A on a test or two, but nothing too crazy, no need to overachieve or raise eyebrows. Whenever a big test was on the horizon, I'd have to pretend to have an emotional reaction—fake some anxiety and self doubt—and watch while my friends struggled to make it, and some not make it at all. I used to study with them and try to drop subtle hints on exactly what we'd be tested on, but after the fourth or fifth time, I felt like they were getting suspicious of me. Maybe I was projecting, but that's how I felt, so I kept my advantage to myself. I didn't feel bad about it either, because in one way or another, help comes when help is given— there's always a trade off. It's basic Base Barter Principle[9]. In any case, I knew that getting caught in a lie that I couldn't

---

[9] *The Base Barter Principle:* Between two interacting entities there's always a level of physical or mental exchange; one's goods for another's services. Although it may go undetected by one, or both parties, and that which is exchanged may not be directly proportional, it exists and transpires nevertheless. Even those who give freely expect to trade their generosity for gratitude.

explain persuasively would only raise suspicion and wouldn't be in anyway helpful to me, so I created some space.

There've been times when I've thought, "you know what, maybe this person just wants to make someone else's day brighter. Make their lives a little easier", but then I vanish, and I wait, and I watch, and I witness firsthand that there's always something the giver gets from the recipient in return.

It was hard to tell if my brother was like this because I didn't see him often, and there's only so much that texts and phone calls can tell me. Things seemed fine and Le'Andre was just as loving as he'd always been, but when he *would* visit me it was like only apart of him was in the room; a cardboard cut out to replace thing. Mentally he was obviously somewhere else. Maybe all the years of looking out for me were just an act, and he wasn't happy with his trade off, or was still waiting for it. I asked him about it once—indirectly —and he told me that he was just intensely involved in his work, probably to a fault. At the time I couldn't imagine doing what he did, living like he did.

"Do you actually like your job, Dre?"

"Is that a thing that people do?" That was a serious question. That's really how he talks almost every time that we have a conversation. It's ridiculous, but it's just as impressive as it is irritating: never ceases to amaze me.

"*Of course.* A lot of people like their jobs. You could do anything you want! Get hired anywhere, start a business— you don't have to be so "intensely involved" in your work that you can't even enjoy when you're not working. You don't have to creep around corners uncovering people's secrets your whole life."

" 'Uncovering people's secrets...' " My brother repeated those three words like they were numbers to a combination lock. "Every conversation you have with someone is potentially a moment when you'll learn something about them that no one else knows. I just do it on purpose and people pay me for it."

There were many times when I just couldn't talk to him, but that's why my girlfriend, Jamie, and I are so melodic together: she understands. She doesn't understand the same way that I do because she hasn't seen what I've seen, but she gets it, and not everyone gets it. People say they get it, they might even think they get it, but they really don't. So once I found someone who actually did, I fastened them to me like a seatbelt because I knew that they would make me feel a little safer on the journey through this world of invisible people and people living invisibly. Jamie understood what mattered, that love is understanding plus effort, and she understood the trade off. She recognized what we gave and received from each other and I loved that—her clarity was sexy. I think I knew her and I would be together long before she did, because I completely trusted her. I showed her how I was able to vanish pretty early on, for some reason everything inside of me said that I could share everything with this person and she didn't disappoint. Ironically, she was the one who arranged my first private investigating job with Ramone, based on the fact that if my brother could do it as a regular person, then I would be a natural. I knew Le'Andre wasn't a "regular" anything. Despite my previous disapproval of the mentally toxic life he was living, there I was, wading through the secret lives of complete strangers just like he did. As it turned out, we were much more alike than I would've hoped. If my life and the lives of others has taught me anything, it's that the most illuminating insight is also the darkest, and soon I would feel a face full of sunshine in the middle of the night.

"Ramone, 'more work' that's what you told me, right? I know you remember that."

"Obviously I remember. I said it. And I told you I'm looking. I've been talking to people that I think would be interested. Jason and Marco think you're great."

"What about talking to people you wouldn't *normally* talk to?"

"If I don't normally talk to someone, then we don't talk." That was a classic Ramone response to someone suggesting an idea that didn't originate from him alone.

"I just don't understand how *no one* else has said yes—do you?"

"So far, everyone's booked up."

"Well, they can't be booked up with someone who can do what *I've* done for you, now can they?"

"So far, the word is that the best exists already. And it's a 'if it ain't broke' kinda business, you know?"

" 'The best'? Better than *me*? How?"

"I don't know, and his people don't know either."

"What do you mean *they* don't know?!"

"I mean what I said: they don't ask questions, they just wait for the results."

"And it's a guy?"

"Asia, you're not serious, right?" My mind is racing so frantically that, until she said my name, I forgot that Jamie was even in the room with Ramone and I. She isn't angry, just taken aback. I'm pacing next to Ramone's kitchen table as he sits, slightly slouched, with his left elbow on the armrest while leaning his head against the index and middle finger of his left hand. He has the countenance of a PhD psychoanalyst, calmly examining the movements of one of their more volatile patients; I look like I'm in a hospital hallway anxiously hoping that the doctor finally has some good news. Worrying is a broken reflex, and I always feel foolish when it's activated, like a nervous tick I have no jurisdiction over erratically fluttering away at its leisure.

The back of the couch is facing us both, so I break the small, repetitive circle of my anxiety-ridden steps, walk over to where Jamie is sitting, lean against it, rest my forearms on top, and look down at my love. Jamie has a cushion behind her head and her feet up, and already has her eyes in my direction when I come into her view.

"Thought I wasn't listening?"

I love her. So much. I knew she was listening—of course she was—she's always listening, and that's possibly what I love the most about her. I know all too well what it's like to not be heard, to be bluntly reminded by those close to you that we live in a silent universe, to be reminded, in a way, of how small you are. I know in the grand scheme of the Earth and in the unknown depths of space, that we're minuscule and none of us actually "matter." The only real significance we have in life is with each other and ourselves, and I find it to be a beautiful privilege to create our own worth. I feel fortunate to have spent a fair amount of time around toxic people, because their true purpose is to confirm the value of those who should be treasured. Jamie's my treasure, and she reminds me daily that I'm hers as well. When she's at her most passionate, she has this way of looking at me like she doesn't see me, but sees into me. As if my eyes, my face— none of it were there. As if none of it matters. She looks at me as if she could see me even if I was invisible.

"Jamie, I'm sorry, but I have to know."

"No, you don't. No one *has* to know anything."

"You're right. I want to."

We both know that she could convince me not to go. By her words and conviction my curiosity could be stifled, but that's not who she is, who we are, have ever been, or ever want to be to each other. I've seen too many relationships that are based on expectation rather than appreciation, on control rather than consideration. Within these interactions lives a constant undercurrent between those involved to endlessly grapple for the upper hand, and what it turns into is not a partnership, but a competition. I vowed to run in the other direction of any relationship remotely resembling that, and when I looked beside me, I found Jamie running from the same.

"I'm sorry, my love."

Jamie sits up and delicately cups my face in hands so soft, and so caring, that I have to close my eyes to complete my next breath.

"You know that we should never feel sorry for doing what we feel we must. I'm here for you, as you are for me."

I tell her that I love her. I use three small words in an attempt to describe something that's inconceivably simpler, more complex, and as old as humanity's very existence. It makes me feel like a toddler who still doesn't know which hand is their strongest, filling a piece of paper with countless squiggly red lines from my favorite crayon—it can't possibly capture what I feel, but it's the best that I can come up with. I apologize to her because I know, even though she's on my side, that she's extremely concerned. However, if there's someone out there who's thought to be better than me—better than a disappearing freak of nature—at getting into spaces that no one else can, then I have to see it for myself. I have to see who's reducing the one thing that's unique about me down to a fraction of its worth. Curiosity leads to one of two destinations: a new way to live, or a new way to die, and my goal is to discover the former since the latter, in time, will come to discover me whether I want it to or not. I take Jamie's left hand off of my face, hold it with both hands, and softly touch my lips to it before I turn around and ask Ramone who I'd be looking for, and where to start looking. The mystery man's name is Damien Jeffries.

More than two months of trying to find someone who has made a career out of being untraceable, led me to Tijuana, then Venice, New York, and ultimately to Las Vegas, where a conversation my brother and I had years ago resurfaced in my mind.

"Never expect anything from anyone, especially not the truth. As long as you remember that anything anyone says to you could be a lie, you'll never be disappointed."

"So, then what makes me different? Unless you believe the same thing about me: that you shouldn't expect the truth from me either?"

"Well, no one's actually *different*—not me, you, anyone—because we're all people, so we all fall victim to the same weaknesses just in different ways. The only thing that makes us different is someone believing that we are, and I believe that about you."

He said that he believed I was different, but I didn't need belief to *know* that he was different because it was so evident to everyone. Now, from inside of his hotel room, I hold up one of the blinds less than an inch from the one below it, and watch him—Le'Andre, my brother, a.k.a. Damien Jeffries—casually stroll around the corner towards a small, unassuming, pale mustard-yellow hotel, as if he's on his way to the next hole on a golf course. He moves as if there's nothing special about him at all. It's still hard to believe that I was an eye-witness when he materialized in a slim, brick-covered alley near downtown Venice. It was in that instance I realized that he had shared an indisputable truth with me: we're all the same, the differences are real in belief alone.

For so long there was nothing I saw in myself to believe in. I couldn't find anything that made me uniquely who I was that I could present to the world, and now that I've finally found it, I can either watch my brother continue to take it from me or I can't. And I can't. No longer will I be a Surrenderist[10] with my life. If I don't have my hands on everything that's within my reach, then I'm placing an aspect of my existence into the hands of another and hoping that their hands are kind. Hope can convince one to buy into anything, but the gamble isn't worth the price paid to play. I

---

[10] Surrenderist Futurism: A Surrenderist accepts that their *present* forecasts the unalterable events of their *future*. Consequently, they would surrender to said forecasted outcome, presuming they could no longer affect it through any fathomable action of their own, or foreseeable action from another. Surrenderist Futurism encapsulates hope, inaction, and acceptance.

haven't come across many pairs of clean hands in my life, because if one is pristine it's only because the other is hidden for a reason.

At any moment he should be walking into the room, so I vanish and move quickly towards the corner furthest away from the door, just behind a small loveseat, that still gives me a clear view. The hotel is arranged oddly, none of the furniture is aligned straight or flush against the wall. It gives me space to stay out of the way, but there's barely room to maneuver if necessary. "Space to hide, but none to move freely"—unfortunately, I can dial *that* number with my eyes closed. *BEEEEP! CLICK!* My brother's keycard unlocks the door, and he makes his way into the room. Pausing after only a few steps, he carefully looks around at how things are arranged with a look of confusion that matches my own, but he changes nothing. He continues towards the bed, drops his small carry-on bag, takes out his phone, and, from what I can see, begins to call someone. With the phone on speaker I can hear it ringing, and after a few rings I hear a phone version of my voice, "Hey, it's Anasia. Hopefully I'm doing something too fun to pick up my phone, so I'll call you right back—that's a lie, I'll probably text you." *BEEP!* Jamie has my cell phone so that she can respond to anyone if it's an emergency. She'll more than likely text Le'Andre back and say that we're out at dinner, or in a movie or something. My brother takes some clothes out of his bag and starts changing, so I lean back, softly sit up against the wall, and avert my eyes. I don't need to see my brother naked. The next thing I hear is the sound of curtains being drawn closed, and then a thud on the bed. I look around from the love seat and Le'Andre is stretched-out diagonally with his eyes closed, I then wait until I hear him snoring before I get up and make my way to the bathroom to wait for him.

It's been about an hour but now I can hear my brother moving about the room, and at some point he'll have to come in here, and that's when I'll end this. This would be right around the time when Jamie would tell me to "go with the flow", to "let things happen", but what's the outcome? Do I sneak out of here, call him and beg him to stop being who he is? It didn't matter that I was thousands of miles away, nimbly his shadow stretched and slithered until it found me.

I wonder how long he's known? Since high school, middle school, elementary? I wonder how many years worth of lies he's fed me while carefully wiping away any loose crumbs from my lips? I wonder if he knows how unexplained brilliance blinds its bystanders? I wonder if he had to see his life flash before his eyes, the way that I did, in order to have his little gift bestowed upon him? I wonder if he had to beg a friend of a friend to leave his hotel room, to please not rape him—*pleading* that he was a virgin—before his body and mind finally allowed him to vanish from sight and make sure that his attacker never attacked any one else again?! No—no, I bet he didn't. I bet he just woke up one morning and was goddamn—the bathroom door is opening. The lights haven't been turned on, but I can hear that Le'Andre's in here. The small backlight from his cell phone comes on, and I can just barely make out his silhouette. He's sitting Indian style on the floor with his back against the wall when his phones backlight light goes off. I already have the shower curtain open, gripping a hunting knife in my hand as tight as the rope to a life raft. I wait and let him get comfortable, then, with feline-like form, I step over the lip of the bathtub and onto the floor to his left. I inhale slowly and fully through my nose, hold my breath before I crouch down low, and then strike.

"Ahhh!" My brother yells louder than I was expecting. I stand up and take a soft step back away from him.

"I didn't want it to be you, you should know that. I wanted it to be someone else—*anyone* else. This isn't what I ever wanted."

"Anasia?!"

"I'm sorry, Le'Andre. I'm sorry about all of this."

"Jesus Christ, Asia! How the—?! Okay, you know what? It's okay. I don't know what this is about or how this is possible, but whatever you think that you want to do right now, we can talk about it. Let's just talk about it, okay? What is it? What do you need from me?"

"What?...What do I...I don't..." I close my eyes tightly and squeeze them as hard as I can. I don't know why, but that question, that one stupid question—I can't think. Everything feels fuzzy. I need a solid thought in my head but everything's like...cotton candy? I feel dizzy, or nauseous, or maybe both —I don't know. It's too dark in here. I reach out, find the bathroom sink, inch my way towards the door, feel around for the light switch, find it and flip it to the "on" position. Once the initial blinding effect wears off, I finally materialize, then the light-show starts: all I see is red—there's blood all over the floor.

"Oh my god, Dre! What did I—*oh my god!* I did this to you?!

"Hey—hey, it's okay, I'll be fine, alright? I'll be fine. But, I'm gonna need your help."

"Oh my god, I'm *so sorry!* I did this to you and—and I'm gonna get help and you'll be fine, and, and you'll be okay."

"Yup, exactly, like it never happened, alright? Just do me a quick favor and grab any clothes I have that I can tie my leg with."

"Yeah, of course—tie your leg, yeah—I'm *so sorry,* Dre, but I'm going to fix this, I promise!"

I'm out of the bathroom like a runner who just heard a starter-pistol fired, but I get stopped mid-sprint when I see the last person that I'd expect to see in this room: Jamie. She's sitting on the edge of the other side of the bed facing the window. I run around the bed to meet her. Her feet are flat on the ground, hands folded in her lap, and she sits with near-perfect posture looking amazing, as always. She asks me if everything is okay.

"Oh my god, Jamie—no, *nothing* is okay, nothing! Wait—wait, what are you doing here?"

"Did you finish things, with your brother?" Her voice isn't at all stern or demanding, but there's an undertone in the way she asks the question. It reminds me of emphatic orchestra conductors swinging their arms in opposite directions, and then simultaneously snapping their fists shut —an action that stops everything.

"No—no he's hurt but he's okay, and it's *my* fault, and I wasn't thinking clearly, and I was just angry, and frustrated— about *a lot* of things—and we need to *help* him, now!"

"You asked me why I'm here, my love."

"Yeah…yeah, right." Jamie stands up, steps close to me, gently holds my face in her hands, and I'm home, instantly, and things aren't as bad as they seem. I close my eyes and I can breathe, finally. The hands are an extension of the heart, and her heart is air and water: they feel like everything I need. We only matter to each other, and her touch alone sings of a timeless simplicity.

"Asia, I'm here for you. I'm here because I know what you've been unfairly burdened with for far too many years and I know that we both know it needs to end. Now." I open my eyes and look into hers hoping they tell me that I'm not hearing what I think I am, but they stand resolute, like two receipts proving that every word was purchased with clear intention—I say nothing.

"Since you first described your brother to me, I suspected that he wasn't merely gifted with extraordinary intelligence. There was something there that I recognized—something familiar—and it wasn't that he was a genius, it's that he was a *Gezien*." She emphasizes "Gezien" as if this word that I've never heard before is supposed to trigger an internal revelation of biblical impact. It doesn't, so I await the rest of the scripture. "I didn't want to assume, which is why I introduced you to Ramone. I figured that if your brother was like you, like I thought he was, then Ramone or someone he knew would've crossed paths with him. I wanted to give you a way to finally rid your life of what's caused you so much pain. A way to finally free yourself. I had hoped that moving the furniture would help." I place my hands on top of hers, remove them from my face, and take a step back.

"I'm going to help my brother."

"Okay. And I am going to help you." Jamie smiles at me warmly, and motions with her arms out to come and give her a hug. Even after everything she's just told me, it would be nice, if only for a moment, to live in the familiarity of her embrace. There's clearly a lot that she's kept locked away from me where she knew I wouldn't think to look. She decided not to disclose, to misinform, to lie, but how does that make her any different from anyone else? How is she different from me, my brother, anyone? I step towards her and she takes a step towards me so that we're close enough for our noses to touch. Leaning closer, she touches her forehead to mine and we wrap our arms around one another. I love her, for better or worse, I love her, and as I'm pressed against her I realize how disarmingly dangerous that is. I should want what's best, but instead, I want what I want. I know that I'm blind, but knowing that I'm blind alone won't be enough to restore my vision. Jamie adjusts herself so that her mouth is next to my ear and she whispers to me.

"And, just as Geziens are able to make themselves invisible, I, on the other hand, am a *Kurettic*, and I can make my self into anything that I wanna be." She lets me go, places her left hand on my shoulder, and I watch as, right in front of my face, she transforms into...me. Without bias, I can attest to the fact that there is nothing more freakishly paralyzing than looking into your own face staring back at you, and knowing that it's on a body that isn't yours.

Jamie pushes me to my right and I collide with the loveseat in the corner, when I look back I see that she's maybe two steps away from entering the bathroom. In her hand is a hunting knife as large as the one that I pushed into Le'Andre's leg, a hunting knife as large as the second one that I had in my back holster. I reach back to confirm the obvious: my knife no longer there. By the time I get to the bathroom door it's already locked, and I bang on it like, well, like I'm trying to save the life of someone that loves me unconditionally.

"Jamie! Jamie, open the door! If you hurt my brother I'll kill you, right now! Jamie! *Jamie!*"

I hear a loud thud, feel the floor vibrate under my feet as something hits it, and I don't have to see it to know what has happened. Someone's dead, and their body just fell for the last time. I step back from the door. I don't know what else to do because either way all of this is my fault. One of the two people that I love the most in this world is dead, right here, in this room. Whoever's still alive is breathing heavily, nearly gasping for air, I can hear them so clearly it's as if the door isn't even there. What have I done?! I know what I'll do next, I know what every bone, and muscle, and every drop of blood in my veins is telling me to do: run. The starter pistol sounds again and I'm off! I get to the room door, push down hard on the handle, and I'm into the hallway, and running faster than I knew I could make my body move. I look behind me and no one's there, no one in front either, and I don't even look for cameras, I'm moving too fast to see them anyway. I vanish and keep pushing my legs and arms to pump faster. As I approach the lobby I have to slow down or I'll run right into the automatic doors before they have a chance to open. I decrease my speed, stop, wait, then accelerate to full speed once again. I'm running so fast that it doesn't feel safe, like if I try to stop or slow down again, I'll end up face down on the hot Las Vegas pavement and that'll be the end of me. I run until my feet hurt, until my legs hurt, until my back hurts, and until I can feel the sweat dripping onto my eye lashes, combining with the tears streaming down my face. I run until I have to inhale and exhale through my mouth, and the air entering my lungs is fresh sandpaper being dragged back and forth all the way down, but I don't stop. I keep going because I know that as long as I'm running then I won't have to deal with everything that's happened. I've heard people say that running away isn't the answer, but that depends on what answers you have to choose from.

UNEVEN 3

I'm obsessed, and it isn't a secret. However, an obsession can keep you alive, and I know that because that's what it's doing for me—it's keeping my mind busy. It's keeping my thoughts from aimlessly wandering into the dark corners of the past, where they can unearth the now shallow graves of memories that were buried alive, but never stopped trying to dig their way to the surface. An obsession can keep one's hands from being idle. It can keep them from doing something that they may regret, like plunging eight inches of stainless steel into their sister's girlfriend's neck and leaving her to die on the bathroom floor of a $15-per-night Las Vegas motel that doesn't even have WiFi. Sometimes an obsession can help more than it hinders. My obsession is information. It's been seven years since I've last seen or spoken to my sister, Anasia, and for the last two years my focus has been to find more, interpret more, figure everything out. This psychopath, Jamie, dates my sister, manages to turn her against me, almost *kills me*, and is mystically still pulling strings in my life from beyond the grave like a harpist. Almost a decade ago, while bleeding on the floor from a flesh wound inflicted by my own flesh and blood, I was just barely able to make out an uttered description of myself that I'd never heard before: *Gezien*. A girl that I'd never met said that was what I was, and that I was just like my sister. After five straight years of looking for my sister under every rock that I could lift, and following every lead I could acquire—whether it was deaf, dumb, or blind—I finally gave up on trying to locate her. I just hoped that wherever she was, she was there by choice.

It was just me now, me and my obsession, since both of my parents died. My mother passed from an autoimmune disease, and my father followed three years later from liver failure. I did what I could for him after mom was gone, but he fell asleep in bottle, after bottle, after bottle, until one day I guess his body just couldn't wake up. The drawback to one numbing their pain is that eventually a line is crossed, and they can no longer feel when they're making it worse. In retrospect, I suppose that's where I get it from. Because of how my parents treated Anasia when she came out, I didn't really expect her to be at either one of their funerals, but I still hoped that she would be. That somehow, from wherever she was, that she would've heard of their passing, and, if nothing else, at least come to let me know that she was okay —that never happened.

All I know now is that we share this ability to vanish, and that this Jamie girl curiously knew that about each of us before we knew it about each other...or did she? Sadly, I never got the chance to *speak* with my sister about how all of this worked for her—I wonder how long she knew? Since high school, middle school, elementary? I wonder how many years of distorted and omitted truths have been exchanged between us, like the earliest merchants arriving at port on sea-beaten, wooden ships to trade silks for spices? I just wanted to see her at her best, and do whatever I could to help her. I wanted her to have the same great experiences that I had in addition to those that would surpass them. I wanted to be an eyewitness at the trial of her successes, knowing that I could testify to them all, but apparently that didn't suffice. So much of what I worked for was to ensure that she knew she was supported, and loved, and cared for, but, as she's evidence of, the easiest thing for people to forget is what you've done for them. Whether between family, friends, or lovers, if not vigilant, we can make the simple pleasure of mutually enjoying and appreciating one another unimaginably complicated. Then again, making a martyr of simplicity, as demanded by complexity, is one of humanity's more overrated and unnecessary attributes.

"I know where I went wrong with her. I don't know that it matters anymore, but after repeatedly replaying the life we shared as siblings in my mind like a song I was trying to learn how to play by ear, I finally saw it: preference. Preference poisons perspective. I made her exempt from what I knew to be true and I paid an expensive price for it. Everything I needed to see was right there in front of me, but I chose to ignore it. I chose to believe what I wanted to be true instead of what I was being shown. I chose to allow preference to poison my perspective. The pattern that's always present was there with her all along: the needless white lies, the uncharacteristic actions and reactions, the avoidance of subjects where one's tracks couldn't easily be concealed, and the overcompensating to mask the anxiety of fabrication. All these indicators spoke clearly and concisely, but I wasn't interested in listening to, or conversing about what I was so clearly being told. I'm not sure what the evolutionary significance of this kind of favoritism is; I don't know what we hope to gain by overlooking faults in one, that we would point out and chastise in another, but the consequences are clear. By perpetuating partiality we inadvertently encourage disharmonizing behavior to intensify; and the hand that adds fuel to the fire will always eventually get burned.

"These are the moments that make breathing feel like a burden, or like a curse placed upon me by a priestess, holding a miniature carved version of my likeness in the palm of her hand. These are the moments when I stand at the crossroads of my memories, look in every direction, and can't see anything else that I could've done differently, or more of, or less of. This is when Human Nature stares at me without eyelids, as an unblinking, mutated science experiment gone cataclysmically wrong, that is seemingly inescapable even in those who share the same parents. I don't understand it, and apparently nothing is more foreign to me. I observe Human Nature and interact with it, yet time and time again, I seem to keep missing the one quintessential piece—or collection of pieces—that will connect me to others and them to me. What am I? At least with Anasia I thought that I could get it right, that I got it right, just this once. These are the moments when I truly don't even feel human but...but you already knew that." I put my mirror face down next to me on my bed, I think even *it* has heard enough from me this early in the morning. If it didn't already have a diagonal crack in the top right-hand corner, it probably would've spontaneously developed one by now from the stress of being my silent, unpaid therapist. It's already after 9 a.m., and I usually can't sleep past seven because of the sun barreling through the thin blinds covering my window. It must be overcast or raining again, because every time I have somewhere to be, it's raining. I hate rushing to get ready, it always frames the following hours with unnecessary tension where none actually needs to exist. I should probably get out of bed now and get going. I press my hands down hard over my eyes, drag the last remnants of tears away, across, and off of my face, and finally roll out of bed.

Two weeks of emailing back and forth have finally secured me a short meeting with Gerald Copper, a YouTuber and Podcast host that I began following more closely over the past six months. From his latest videos, he doesn't seem to be much older than I am—a bald, slender-faced man, with smaller than usual eyes and larger than usual eyebrows, that sat just above brown, horn-rimmed glasses that never left his face. He and his father used to have a joint channel that focused on decoding the Bible and other religious texts, which me and my college roommate, Adam, were very much captivated with when we were younger. Adam and I only speak via text message maybe three or four times a year, and usually not at length, but it was Adam who actually sent me the link to Gerald's page, letting me know that he was still at it after all these years. Coincidentally, Gerald is now into more mythological writings and trying to connect them to what would conversely be considered "real life" events. Recently, he discussed on both his podcast and YouTube channel a newly discovered Greco-Roman text translated from African writings found in southern Cameroon. Along with accounts of more notably recorded figures like zombies, vampires, werewolves, ghosts and giants, there were specific references to "invisible men" who were born "Gezien". The writers of the text described this classification as basically having an exceptional birth defect. In the episodes that followed, Copper didn't go into much more detail about the Gezien defect specifically, but often seemed to allude to knowing more about the subject if anyone was interested. Even via email he didn't want to discuss much more either, but now here he is approaching me—only 13 minutes late—to speak outside of a coffee shop. I wave him down, he shakes my hand, and takes a seat across from me. We exchange the normal pleasantries, I thank him for meeting me and offer to get him something from inside, but he lifts a metallic cup that he brought with him and remarks that he's good for now.

"We can get right into it, if you want—it's Damien, right? I'm the worst with names, sorry."

"Damien—yeah, you got it. And sure, sounds good. I guess then, just picking up from where we left off in the emails, the Gezien thing was just really interesting to me, obviously. But I couldn't find much of anything online though."

"Weird, right? I had the same problem. All the info that I was able to get was from a listener to the show. Get this: he had a copy of the actual book."

"From Ancient *Greece?*"

"Ay, it looked pretty damn old to me! Plus he had the African version that it was *translated from,* and it had these illustrations—it was pretty nuts. And he wanted nothing from me, not even his name mentioned, just said that people should know about this just like anything else, but in a responsible way."

"Responsible way?"

"According to him, the book has secrets that could get into the wrong hands"

"Hm, okay. So, you can't run a few shows or videos about it?"

"He asked me not to."

"Really?"

"Yeah, it was a little weird—trust me—but he said he'd give me more info soon, and then I could really get into it. But that if anyone reached out asking specifically, that I could tell 'em a little more. You've been the only one."

"Lucky me." I chuckle, trying to keep the mood light.

"Yeah, it looks that way." Copper chuckles as well. Naturally all of this could be fake, but so far he seems relatively legit. If anyone's making this stuff up, it's going to be his mystery contact, who supposedly has ancient secrets that have only been seen by select people. That's not suspicious at all.

"Well, what else can you tell me? I think the last thing I remember being able to catch on the show about it was that Gezien was like a birth defect? That seemed different." I'm not sure if I come off as a bit too excited, but Copper literally glances back over his shoulder, and then looks past me just over *my* shoulder. I keep a straight face, but he's acting like we're in a detective movie from the '70's or something. Moving his chair forward, he rests his forearms on the table and leans in towards me.

"Just—let's keep our voices down, okay? I know all of this sounds like *science fiction* or some rehashed *fairytale*—most would probably regard this as some ancient entertainment rather than "proper" mythology, but this *guy*, he was dead serious, alright?" I lower my voice and lean in as Copper did.

"Yeah, no, absolutely—I get it."

"Well, not yet you don't." He's literally told me nothing at all, but it's obvious that whatever he *thinks* he knows already has him convinced. He looks back over his shoulder again, and I take a look myself to see if anything's there—why not? "So, yeah, these texts are supposed to describe this birth defect called 'Gezienism', and it's the birth defect that everyone wishes they had. Tribes would test young kids *harshly* to see if their bodies would react and if they would, well, disappear. If they did, they were immediately revered. On the spot they would go from *children*, to gods walking amongst men."

"And this guy just showed you all this?"

"Yeah, he showed me the illustrations from Cameroon, and was explaining the Greek breakdown, and the translations, and everything." This could all be a coincidence, and I know it could. Adam sends me a link, I listen, and subconsciously I'm hoping to hear something that applies to me. So I alter the way I listen, and unknowingly become more subjective without trying—it's basic psychology. At the time I had been digging for almost two years, and I was still in the dark unable to find anything at all. When this fell in my lap, it was like the door opened up just enough for a golden, sliver of light, to enter the room and show me a way out. But, where was this really leading me?

"So, you speak Classical Greek as well?" I'm not asking to be condescending, I'm actually generally interested, but instantly it's clear that Copper takes offense. His leg is twitching so hard I can feel it shaking the table.

"What, you think I've been looking over my shoulder so I can stretch my neck?! Listen, the *last thing* this guy told me was that there wasn't *any* documentation that said this birth defect *didn't* keep popping up in people. He said these Geziens, are still here—anywhere! You understand how *insane* that is, right? This is actually *real* and these things are out here! And honestly, I don't care how it sounds because I know what he showed me, alright?! Everyone thinks the truth is this diamond buried so far underground that it needs to be *mined* to the surface, when in reality it's gold. It's sitting in a shallow riverbed, glittering in the sun right there in front of us, and we'll walk right past it if we don't look down, or if we don't actually know what it is we're looking for." I say nothing. There's a time to listen, and that time should never be wasted. Copper leans back in his chair, takes off his glasses, puts them on the table, and slowly rubs his face in one swipe starting at his forehead and stopping at his chin. He picks his glasses back up, returns them to sitting on the bridge of his nose, and leans towards me again. "This guy—Danny—was supposed to meet me again a week and half ago, but I couldn't get a hold of him, alright? He said he had proof of reports, and sightings over recent years. Who knows, maybe he knows *too much,* maybe they got to him first—I got no idea. Why do you even want to know about this stuff anyway?" I already had a prepared answer to this question, because I knew that it had to come up at some point. Ironically, it wasn't far from the truth.

"Ay, man, I get it, okay? And, trust me, I wouldn't have sent you a million emails if I didn't take this seriously. But I'll always ask the obvious questions, because I know the answers are seldom obvious—that's just me, bro. And I'm actually asking because I think that my *sister* might be—like you said—one of these *things.* I've either seen or almost seen her do some pretty odd stuff, so I'm just trying to find out as much as possible."

"Your sister..." It wasn't a question, not quite a definitive statement either, more of acknowledgement of an incorrect answer given by a student who had no idea what class they were in. All I could do is try to reroute my misstep. "Well, I haven't seen her since we were *kids* and—"

"The *one thing* this guy told me for sure was that all over these texts it spoke about siblings, and how the defect was always shared by the first three children." I don't consider myself to be a great liar, but I know a thing or two about lies because I know a thing or two about the truth. What most would classify as a lie, I see a little differently now, it's all a part of *Falsehood Theory*. A lie is the truth had circumstances been different. It's a believable alternative to a provable fact or sincere point of view, so all that *really* separates a lie from the truth is a thorough imagination. In essence, lies and truths are in the same category—they're both stories one chooses to accept or deny. Unfortunately, in this particular example, as I sit across from a man who I've just met, whose face is now *embossed* with anxiety, there is not one believable alternative that I can think of quick enough to diffuse this situation. I open my mouth to say something—anything— that will break the silence, but before a single syllable escapes, Copper yanks the lid off of his cup, and launches the coffee in my face. It burns and I can't see, but I can hear the screech of metal chair legs scraping abrasively on the concrete before I feel the edge of the table collide with my stomach like a meteorite . I regain enough of my breath and get my eyes cleared in time to see Copper slam his car door, and recklessly tear off into traffic ahead of a bus. The bus driver has to slam on both the breaks and horn with equal force in order to avoid being involved in an accident. And I'm going to need more napkins.

I would usually wait for the bus and take a quick 15-minute ride to my apartment a few blocks away, but after that Gerald Copper fiasco, even a 35-minute walk on my bad leg sounds like an unparalleled idea right now. I slide the zipper on my jacket up until it stops at my collar, this way it hides my failed attempt at ridding my shirt of the coffee that it's now stained with. Unavoidably, the short beard that I started growing a few weeks ago now carries the faint aroma of cream and sugar. I check the mirror once more, put my sunglasses back on, walk out of the coffee shop's bathroom, and close the door behind me. As I try to make my way out as discreetly as possible, I'm addressed by one of the baristas: a short, slim, attractive girl with long, black hair braided down to her lower back, she's maybe in her early 30's, but she could pass for much younger.

"Did you *know* that guy sitting here? Because I think he might be *clinically* insane." I slow my pace, but don't completely stop moving.

"Uhh, not really. Was just supposed to be sort of a quick business meeting thing." She walks around the table to the left and picks up the chair that Copper pushed away from the table. I continue around to the right of the table.

"Didn't go so well, huh?" The chair slips out of her hands just as she was trying to align it to the correct position adjacent to the table, and hits the ground loudly. "Oops, sorry." I chuckle and smile sympathetically.

"No, you're fine. And yeah, no, didn't *quite* go as expected." I adjust the chair across from the girl where I was previously sitting, smile politely, and continue to move away from the table, away from the coffee shop, and into the direction of my apartment. I have far too much on my mind right now for small talk.

As is customary, I'm replaying the conversation between myself and Copper in my head as I make a left and cross the street at the first stoplight after the coffee shop. I know more than I did before I got there, now I just have to make sense of it and compartmentalize the new information. He was terrified of the danger that I posed to him without knowing anything about me for certain, but apparently that's the effect of even *possibly* being a Gezien. He regards the truth as gold and I regard it as non-existent—not a part of the conversation that's immediately relevant, but all insight is invaluable and all perspectives can help lead to clarity. Then there are the books that no one with any real expertise has seen. There's no way to immediately confirm their validity, and the holder of said books appears to have either chosen to go M.I.A., or the choice was made for him. "Danny" is who I really need to be talking to. How did he come across these texts? Who had them before he did? Why come forward with them now? Assuming the texts are authentic, what's he *getting* out of all this? There has to be something. There always is. All people, at any given moment, are either ruled by want or need, so I always start there to make sense of one's motives that are otherwise a mystery. I observe, theorize, vanish, and then confirm if I was correct, but it's actually been years now since vanishing has been a necessity. For the most part, I've memorized the recipe to the shaken cocktail served cold over crushed ice that is human fidelity.

I thought walking would help me think clearer—it usually has that effect—but I need to sit somewhere, take some notes, get some visual aids for myself, and see what other keywords I can possibly use to dig something up online. I'd even hit a library at this point. What I definitely know is that I can't go home and hope to get any of this done, because trying to accomplish anything remotely constructive while in my own apartment is next to impossible. At home all I can manage to focus on is eating, drinking, sleeping, meditating, and relaxing—"working" doesn't even get an honorable mention. There's a burger spot on 7th that I'll probably end up stopping at as usual, mostly because I can loiter there for hours and no one bothers me. They don't even flinch when I sit at a booth with entire meals that I bring in from somewhere else. I love that place.

It's getting chilly outside now, so walking around with my jacket zipped all the way up finally feels comfortable. As I make a right onto 7th, I'm not only greeted by the familiar sight of the obnoxious neon burger sign for Walter's B&F's (burgers and fries), but a straight-on view of the sunset. The simple pleasure of mutually appreciating, and enjoying another person is one of the countless magical moments of impermanence that is often dangerously undervalued, just like this sunset. I realize that "sunsets" and "sunrises" aren't actually a real thing. It isn't the *sun* that's setting lower or rising higher on the horizon, but a specific spot on the Earth that's *rotating* towards or away from it's light—I think that better captures the magnitude of what's being witnessed. I'm not watching the sunset or the sunrise, I'm watching the Earth move. I take a step closer to the curb on my left, stop, lean up against a parking meter and look up. The boundless ceiling above me is smeared with broad pastel strokes of yellow, orange, and violet as far east and west as my eyes can wander, all arranged by the timeless rotation of a relatively small, blue planet, twirling its way around an even more timeless star. This is an inexpressible, fleeting moment in time, and I'll never see this one particular sunset ever again, just like my sister. Everything is borrowed. All of this is taking place while I'm trying to find out what exactly *I* am, and I feel like there's a metaphor somewhere here to be recognized, or maybe I've already recognized it. I need to sit down and think.

Once inside Walter's, I'm reminded of what day and hour it is: dinner time on a Friday, which equals few open seats at the place with arguably the best burgers in the city. I walk slowly in the direction of the register—honestly, barely moving at all—as if I actually plan on ordering something, all the while hoping to see a booth open up where I can sit down. As I'm carefully surveying the dining area to my right, over my left shoulder I hear my song of salvation "Hey, we have to *go*. If we don't leave now, we'll never find parking." Hallelujah! I swing around to my left, wait for the group of three to leave, and claim my prize—dropping myself down into the long seat, nearly crushing my cell phone tucked in my back pocket in the process. I take my phone out of my pocket, put it in on the table, and let my body slouch down until my feet touch the seat across from me. I'm not sure how I thought this day would go, but it definitely wasn't like this. I pick up my phone, open Google, and try to incorporate the little information I received from Copper into my usual black hole of keywords: "Greco-Roman Gezien myth texts", "ancient texts of Cameroon", "Gezien siblings in Roman myth", "Gezien siblings in African myth", "Gezienism birth defect", "ancient Gezienism". Every search either gives me no results, or three pages of any random thing associated with Greece, Rome, Africa, or myth, all of which I've read a million times before. I lock my phone, and at this angle, I can see my reflection perfectly in the blank, black screen, and I look at myself. This is pointless. I put my phone down, and defeatedly rest both of my hands on top of my head. Now that my eyes are no longer glued to a back-lit screen, I realize there's someone different sitting in the booth in front of me: what appears to be a homeless man with a delivery-size box of pizza, leisurely having a slice of his pie while holding a small, clear cup of water in the other hand. The man's hair is nearly completely gray with only leftover spots of a darker color—black or brown—near the root. His sun-beaten skin has an orange hue to it which is only a few shades darker than the orange in his jacket, and his face is lined with deep wrinkles that resemble drought-stricken riverbeds surrounded by tumbleweed. The man looks up from his pizza in my direction and it's too late for me to look away. I nod at him casually and he does the same, but he attaches a friendlier-than-expected smile as well. I look back down at the table knowing what's coming next: this man is going to start a conversation, and this time, I'd love to be incorrect about my assumption. Generally, I've grown to hate being right about people, I'd much rather be wrong. I'd rather be greeted with the confirmation of my ignorance and shown the world to be brighter than I judged it to be, than chauffeured by the testimony of my wisdom which only proves that the world exists in the darkness I always thought that it did.

"You doing alright this evening?" The man in front of me begins right on time.

"Not too bad, you?" There's no reason to be rude. I have nowhere to be.

"Oh, I'm doing just fine, just as good and fine as anybody."
I nod at his statement, but don't respond. 'Not too bad, you?'
was all I had in my kitchen to contribute. What's surprising is
that I can't remember ever seeing a homeless person look as
thoroughly happy as this man does. Come to think of it, I've
been in the presence of many people who were *far* from
homeless who didn't look as happy as this man does. He was,
of course, sitting in front of a whole pizza by himself. He
starts up again.

"You know it's never as bad as you think it is—that's the
one thing I've learned—you just have to keep going. Just
keep pushing. I haven't had a home in, well, almost 11 years
now, and at times I thought I wanted to die, just end it all,
but I didn't, and I'm glad I didn't. Just have to keep going."

"Yeah...yeah, definitely." A little too much personal
information to share with a stranger, in my opinion, but then
again I guess we're all strangers to each other until we
choose to share something personal—funny how that works.
I push myself up from my well-defined slouch. His statement
was oddly idoneous for my particular frame of mind; and he
must have noticed my slight peak in interest.

"I'm Daniel by the way. What's your name?"

"Damien." Why not bring the old code name back for this
random person I'll never see again in my life?

"Damien? Nice to meet you. I had a buddy of mine who
was friends with a Damien, but that was in Taiwan—*long*
time ago. I was in Taiwan for, oh, about eight years, and my
kids are still there, just don't get to see them as much as I'd
like. Taiwan's a hell of a country. No rules in that place, but
reminds me a lot of Mexico in that way, actually. You sure can
getaway with a lot, you know what I mean?" Why would he
think that *I* know what *he* means? Why even use that as a

colloquialism in this case? Are there *that* many people who've been to both Taiwan and Mexico that would be able to confirm that *extremely* specific parallel?

"No, uh, I hadn't heard that about Taiwan."

"Oh, *yeah*, at least when I was there, like I said, that was a while back—*long time*—but it didn't strike me as the kind of place to really change, you know? But, now I'm here, just living each day. It's not easy being homeless, but it's a lot easier here than in Taiwan." I nod again. I'm courteous to a fault with people that are older than I am, at this point I'm just hoping there's a point to this story, but I seriously doubt it. And, he's *not* finished. "What's 'homeless' in the West is just 'making it by' in Taiwan—the hard part is being invisible. Can you imagine that? No one even sees me here, other than maybe the police, and sometimes even they look *right* through me. I know that I'm nothing to nobody. Can you imagine what that's like? People not even seeing you when you're right in front of 'em? If I don't see being invisible as freedom, I'll see it as a death sentence. I'll see it as the signature on my suicide letter. But, you know being invisible ain't too bad if you get to be invisible whenever you want, right?" I sit up even straighter, and can't help my eyebrows from scrunching together at the man's last few words. "Invisible whenever you want." What the hell was he saying? He grabs his pizza box and his cup of water and slides out of the booth before I can gather my thoughts. I must be putting things into my own head now, too much talk about Geziens for the day.

"Have a good one, buddy."

"Yeah—thanks, you too."

I watch as the man walks out the door, past the large display window, and out of sight. I briefly look down at the table "This has been the weirdest day," and then look back at the display window to see that the homeless man's returned. He smiles at me knowingly, looks to his left and his right, waves, winks, and then vanishes—he *vanishes*. Vanishes, like he disappears. It's impossible! I get out of the booth and drag my limp—as it begs for me to stop—out of the restaurant and onto the sidewalk, and I don't see him or his orange jacket anywhere. He's actually gone. He's like me. How? I walk back inside to get my phone, and purposefully ignore the confused stares that I'm getting from almost every one of the people sitting around me. When I get back to the table there's a napkin beside my phone with something written on it:

"YEAH, SO DANNY IS PRETTY DRAMATIC. HE KNOWS A LOT THOUGH. FIGURED YOU TWO SHOULD MEET SINCE YOU MET GERALD. I'M HEADING BACK TO ROSARITO NOW. WE SHOULD GET TACOS ONE DAY AND CATCH UP.

 - ASIA

Tacos, I love tacos.

FOR HIRE: MASTER

She's struggling to breathe, but I need her to be strong. I need her to fight like I've fought. I need her to stay alive, because if she dies now then all of this would be pointless. Death is silent and she needs to hear this—not that I'm saying anything verbally. Some choose to talk their way through a murder. They yell into their subjects face or whisper threats into their ear, but I prefer a more organic soundtrack. If I speak, it will have a purpose. People can tell you exactly who they are without saying a word and I hate wasting my breath, especially in moments like these when its importance becomes so drastically clear. I look deep into her eyes and try not to blink—I don't want to miss even a second of this. When all control is lost to another, the eyes are no longer solely a window to the soul, they are a ballet. They dance and twist, desperately searching for meaning, contorting themselves to beg for the answers to questions they've never asked. I'm able to see more than her soul, I see all that it never will be, and it's a promise that is kept over and over. I let the heat from my heart rise through my hands, and the flame swallows everything that it touches.

He's so unwaveringly strong. It's as if God gave birth to a child that Satan fathered, and now that creation has gotten a hold of me—I didn't know such power existed. I was scared initially, but the fear has given way to something else, something more enveloping: desperation. I'm trying to hold on. I'm trying only to make it to the next moment of life that I can, because the future and past have lost all relevance, I just want more of right now. I have to watch his mouth to know if he's speaking because all I can hear is my pulse—a percussionist being pushed to play harder and faster by an overbearing mentor. His hands squeeze my throat tighter. The hands are an extension of the heart, and his heart is fresh leather and carved wood: life twisted by the desires of humanity into something dead, but now a functional work of art. I look deep into his eyes and try not to blink, I don't want to miss even a second of this. I have given him control, I have given him everything that I know, and it was everything that I wanted it to be: a death both seen and experienced—a death worth remembering. This is why I hired him, so he could do what I couldn't: kill me.

FOR HIRE: APPRENTICE

He's crying heavy tears, the type of tears that change the way you breathe—tears that make each breath a gasp, tumbling over a gasp, tumbling over another gasp. He must realize now that this won't be easy. Death, like life, is only fair in its unfairness, and this revelation is beautifully written all over his face. The pain must be kicking in, so his natural instinct to fight back becomes like a toddler throwing a tantrum, kicking and screaming on the floor to be released. They want to play too —but no-no, this is grown-up time. Adults play differently, they no longer innocently pursue joyful recreation—life involves too much responsibility. There's too much to lose, too much to gain—it's about the escape now. Playtime for adults is about running as far away from the person they've become, in order to find—even for a moment—the person they truly are. This is why I'm here: to push the reset button; and death is the only experience truly equivalent to birth.

I look deep into his eyes and smile at him with mine. I can see everything he's running from, and I show him everything he'll find once he finally gets away. He understands and I know it—his eyes show me that he does—no need to waste words with me. The tips of my fingers become silk when I wipe the tears from his face, and the knife I push into his neck and pull out swiftly is the last kiss he will ever feel.

1

She's acting as if she doesn't see what's happening to me. There's no way she could miss me gasping in between tears like a toddler, or the fact that I'm now a melting iceberg—the layers of who I am and who I once was crumbling, and falling away from me into the subzero waters of my sustenance. It's almost as if she's not judging me—I never knew such tenderness existed. I was scared initially, but the fear has given way to something else, something more enveloping: disappointment. I should fight this, I should show her I'm stronger than this, show *myself* I'm stronger than this—show the world that I can beat it!—but I know that's not really what I want. I just want to get out of here. I've had enough. This is where I should be, even though it hurts, even though it isn't easy, she makes it seem so elegant. Each cut brings pain, but the pain is followed by a release, like bearing a child—Death's subtle way of mimicking Life.

My head feels heavy. She lifts my chin up, looks deep into my eyes and smiles at me with hers, and for the first time I see freedom. It speaks to me and it says my name like a crown being placed on the head of the heir to the throne— I'm recognized. She wipes the tears from my face and her fingertips are Understanding, erasing all I've ever been ashamed of. Something then pinches my neck—the pain prior to the release—and I remember that this is why I hired her, so she could do what I couldn't: kill me.

Sean Aeon

DARKER VISION

At around 9:30 p.m., on an overcast night outside of a 12-floor apartment building, the back and forth swishing of plastic grocery bags can be heard as Naisyn Sage runs towards the apartment she shares with her boyfriend, Jamar Hopsin. As she gets to the entrance of the building, she struggles to get her keys out of the left pocket of her burgundy skinny jeans while using her right hand. She could just switch the three bags she's holding with her left hand over to her right, but after running on and off for a block, her fingers are now intertwined with the thin, plastic handles of the bags like the twisted vines growing up the side of her building. Finally, she maneuvers herself to just the right angle to get her hand to the bottom of her pocket, shimmies her keys out and hurries through the set of glass doors. Naisyn's sneakers squeak on the tile of the lobby floor as she jogs to the elevator and taps on the up arrow repeatedly before stopping to look up at the digital floor-indicator. It slowly counts down from nine, pausing momentarily and dinging like hotel concierge bells on each subsequent floor number. After four dings, it stops and starts ascending back up through the numbers. Naisyn's jaw drops as she's immediately struck by disbelief and frustration simultaneously, "is this real life, right now?!" She emphatically looks over both of her shoulders—knowing that no one else is there—to see if there are any witnesses to this madness. She raises her middle finger up to the elevator—causing the group of copper bangles on her wrist to race down her forearm—switches the grocery bags to her left hand and takes off for the door underneath the red exit sign leading to the stairs.

Leaping up the concrete steps two at time, Naisyn arrives at her floor in minutes, swings open a door with a large, yellow 8 printed on it, and speed walks towards her and her boyfriend's unit. Moving too quickly to unlock the door, the key jams as she narrowly misses the key hole, causing them to fall out of her hand. Like a flash of lightning, she swipes them out of the air before they're even close to hitting the ground, "Nope!" This time she deliberately angles her house key at the edge of the keyhole and makes sure that it slips right in. Once in the doorway, she slides the grocery bags on the floor towards their dining table. She doesn't immediately see Jamar. He's not to her right in the kitchen, and when she pushes open the already ajar bedroom door, he's not in there or in the adjoining bathroom. A flash of worry causes her face to tighten, but he has to be home. "Jay, baby, where are you? If we're gonna go, I think we gotta go n—." She finally sees him. Through the living room, the blinds are just open enough to catch his silhouette sitting on the railing of their balcony. The railing is about five feet high, so it isn't exactly easy to get on top of. As Naisyn walks in his direction, she notices a pill bottle on the coffee table next to a bottle of tequila and the TV remote. She picks up the pill bottle and rattles it before looking inside—only two left—and the bottle of tequila only has enough for maybe a modest shot or two. She gets to the entrance of the balcony, moves the off-white blinds and the sliding door to her right, and stands in the entrance leaning on her left shoulder—she's already concerned.

"Jay, baby, you, uh, you alright?" He doesn't react. He doesn't move at all. She can't even tell if he's breathing. He's sitting with his head straight, his hands holding on to the railing on either side of him, with the lights of the city twinkling in the distance—the scene could be an album cover.

"What are we doing here, Nai? Like really, what is this…" Jamar turns his head to his right just enough to bring Naisyn into his peripheral, "…actually?" She nods her head slowly—stoically—and reaches over to adjust two of her bracelets. She'll tread as carefully as she can for as long as time permits.

"How about you come down off the railing and, you know, we can—we can talk about it. Looks like you almost got through a whole bottle while I was gone." Jamar sighs—does she not understand him? Is she not taking him seriously? And he turns his head to his right again.

"Did you hear what I said?"

"Yeah, no, I heard you." Naisyn reluctantly has to play along if she's going to get him down in time. She pulls her phone out of her back pocket and checks the time. "What do you mean, 'what is this?'?"

Jamar swings his right arm out towards the horizon.

"This! All of this! We just wake up, eat, work, have sex, pay bills, go to sleep, and then…then we just do it all over again.

"Is that how you feel about us, that we're a, a *chore?*" Of course that isn't what he meant, but that's his superpower: saying things that unintentionally, and deeply, offend the people he wants to keep in his life.

"No, I—"

"Because if that's what we are to you—"

"IT'S NOT ABOUT US!" He didn't mean to yell as loud as he did, he just wanted to stop her from saying anything about them that wasn't true. Taken aback by the unusual outburst, Naisyn adjusts her posture and clears her throat. Jamar itches the back of his head.

"I'm sorry. It's not about us, I...I promise." Naisyn's face changes. Something's wrong with him, something must have happened.

"You took all of the pills?"

"Did I? They didn't help."

"Jamar, *what's* going on?"

He tilts his head up towards the sky, exhales audibly, then says nothing.

"Because I *really* think we have to go. Like we should get our stuff and get outta here, now! I heard people at the store saying—."

"Who *cares* what they're saying?"

Naisyn takes two small steps onto the balcony so that she's standing just inside the doorway, and then stops.

"You really don't sound like yourself."

"You don't ever just want to die, Naisyn? Finally get it over with?"

She freezes in place, stunned at the question—she can't blink, or breathe, or move at all. He couldn't have said what she thought she heard. Jamar looks at her over his right shoulder.

"Just finally be done with all of...everything? Done with all of the hate, and the prejudice, and the worry, and the suspicion, and...they hate us. You know that. I know you do.

They hate us everywhere—that's what they said at the store, right? They hate us and want us out of here, right?"

Despair drapes over Naisyn's face, and her lip quivers. She takes another step closer to Jamar.

"I'm coming over to you, okay?" Two more small, quiet movements forward.

"Just stay there, Nai. I don't know…I don't know what I might do. I'm tired. I'm…tired of apologizing for being myself. I'm—"

"You know you don't ever have to—"

"I'm tired!" Jamar rubs his forehead, and lowers his voice.

"I'm tired. I'm tired of all of it. I'm tired of fighting for us, for…defending us…defending our right to be alive. It's every…single…day." He looks down and shakes his head. It's not that he *can't* keep living like this, but he doesn't want to and there's no escape. Naisyn continues to quietly move closer to him, like a jungle cat approaching its prey. She can feel his pain, and she needs to be by his side if she's going to help him.

"I know. I know it's a lot—*you* know I know—and we're going to get through this, through everything, just like…just like we always have."

Jamar closes his eyes and takes a deep breath. He doesn't want to deal with what they've always dealt with, he knows that life can be better than normal—he wants something better. "I'm almost to you. I'm almost right by your side where I'm supposed to be."

"I don't know if that's a good idea. I don't…" Jamar sighs and looks down at the street below, "I don't know anymore…and you're not gonna be happy."

Naisyn is only a step away from him now. She loved how big their balcony was when they first moved in, but she never noticed how truly big it was until she had to use her five foot, three inch frame to tip toe across it. "Everything's gonna be okay. I'm gonna help you back onto the balcony, and we're gonna get outta here, and we'll be good—better than good." Finally within arms reach, she gently places her hand on his back and can feel his heartbeat. Slow, steady thumps knock two at a time against her palm—it knows where home is. Peering around at him for the first time, she can now see the front of his body: Jamar's shirt is spattered with blood—a lot of it. Naisyn's eyes get extremely wide and she mutes a gasp before she can completely let it out. Her chest rises and falls noticeably as the shock surges through her entire body. She's close enough to him now that he can feel the tension that's gripped her. He hates it when she feels like this, but this time it was unavoidable.

"Told you."

"Jamar, what…"

"I won't apologize, Naisyn." He looks her in the eye and rests his right hand on her face. "I won't apologize for defending us. They think they can say whatever they want about us. Kill *us* in the street like we're dogs?" Jamar averts his eyes, bites his bottom lip, and shakes his head before returning to look at her. "Nah, those days are long gone. We belong here as much as they do, probably more so."

Naisyn gently places her hand on top of the one Jamar has on her face.

"What did you do, my love?" He proudly raises his chin along with his chest.

"I stood my ground."

Naisyn looks down and away from Jamar, then back to face him, nodding her head understandingly. All she can do is hope he doesn't mean what she thinks he does.

Earlier that same evening, Jamar is walking down the street as he approaches three white men walking in the opposite direction. They all seem to be in their late 20's to mid 30's, and their speech and laughter is a little too animated for them to be sober. One has on a camo-print hunting hat, the other a trucker hat with a shark on it, and the third is hatless. He's not in the mood to deal with anything or anyone that doesn't concern him, so he puts on his sunglasses, pulls out his phone, and swipes his finger around the screen to make it appear as if he's occupied. Hunting Hat taps Shark Hat and points at Jamar. Jamar's now concealed eyes are watching them closely. Shark Hat's face twists like a bitter taste just invaded his mouth and he shakes his head and spits on the ground behind him. Hatless looks over at the two others, confused.

"Y'all know him?"

Hunting Hat rolls his eyes at the obvious question.

"God, you just don't know nothing, huh?"

Hatless shrugs innocently before Shark Hat barks at him.

"Who the hell you think?! That's the new bastard nobody wants here!"

Hunting Hat rubs his hands together.

"And now we get to show him that his kind ain't goddamn welcome."

Jamar watches as they talk amongst themselves while they get gradually closer. He can't hear every word, but from what he can catch, it sounds like his time is about to be wasted. He's ready. Shark Hat is the first to open his mouth.

"Hey bud, you're new here, right?"

Jamar nods at the question without breaking his stride.

"Yeah, haven't been here too long. Y'all have a good night."

The three men angle themselves so that they block Jamar from trying to move to the opening to his left. Now Hunting Hat has something to say.

"In a hurry?"

Jamar puts his phone in his back pocket while keeping his eyes on the three men.

"Long day—you know how it is—if you'll excuse me."

None of the men move. Hatless looks over at Hunting Hat and Shark Hat, and sees they haven't taken their eyes off of Jamar, so he also looks back over at Jamar. Shark Hat folds his arms.

"Maybe you should getta new job...*in a new state.*"

Jamar is a statue with his hands still resting in his pockets. He says nothing. Hatless ping pongs his head back and forth following the exchange between Jamar and his two friends— he just wants to get to the bar. Meanwhile, Hunting Hat adds on to Shark Hat's last statement.

"Yeah, getta new job and don't *ever* come back."

Jamar nods his head.

"Yeah, I think I'll probably leave when I'm ready, but thanks for the suggestion though." He moves to his right to try to step past the men again. Hunting Hat and Shark Hat shift to block him again, moving Hatless along with them. Hunting Hat taps Shark Hat on the shoulder.

"Maybe we ain't make ourselves clear enough, Gun."

"Hm. Maybe I knock his teeth out, and then he'll understand that he ain't welcome." Shark Hat punches his right fist into his left palm in an attempted threatening gesture. Jamar takes his left hand out of his pocket and itches his face, mildly confused.

" 'Gun'...so, your full name's probably 'Gunther' then, right?"

Shark Hat lifts his chin up pridefully. Looks like Jamar got it right on his first guess. He then looks over at the still anonymous Hunting Hat.

"Okay, so *you're* trying to threaten *me* with a guy named Gunther?" Jamar scans all three of the men, then quietly chuckles to himself. "That actually makes me feel a whole lot better, thank you."

A fist flies towards Jamar's face. His right hand escapes from his pocket to catch and grip the fist just short of his cheek bone. Shark Hat, a.k.a. Gunther, tries to yank his fist back, but Jamar isn't letting go, and for a moment the two other men are stunned at the powerful display of speed and strength. Hunting Hat snaps out of it and swings at Jamar, but with one tug, Jamar slides Gunther in front of himself like a glass patio door. Gunther absorbs the full impact of the punch instead—Hunting Hat yells.

"Shit! Gun?!"

Hatless's jaw falls to the floor.

"I'll be damned."

Jamar then yanks Gunther to the ground—spinning him behind himself—by the fist that he's still got a grip on and horse kicks him in the face. Using his left hand he punches Hunting Hat in the jaw, grabs him by his shirt and yanks him close. Jamar opens his mouth and four long incisor fangs ready themselves to plunge into Hunting Hat's neck. Hatless is baring witness to a nightmare his brain can barely comprehend.

"Ho-ly shit."

With his hands and whole body shaking with fear, Hatless reaches into his pocket and struggles to pull out his phone. Jamar looks over, hisses at him viciously, and Hatless takes off sprinting into the night. Jamar's pupils, iris', and scleras all turn pitch black as he once again prepares to bite into Hunting Hat. His fangs are as bright as high beams in the dark.

Back at the apartment, after listening in frozen suspense and disbelief, Naisyn steps away from Jamar and looks at him with her eyes begging.

"Please tell me you didn't."

"I told you you wouldn't be happy."

Naisyn breaks into a nervous pace, then looks at her phone and realizes how much time they've burned through.

" *'I'm so sorry, Naisyn!'* That, that's what you meant to say —Jesus! Not everyone is just okay with *vampires* in their backyard! We need to—it doesn't matter—we just need to go."

Jamar hangs his head low—he knows how bad this is; he knows he wasn't thinking about the love of his life when he bit into that idiot a few hours ago. What he was thinking about was taking back control, and he did. Now, he wonders if it was worth it—worth that fleeting moment of dominance —because he always has trouble rightfully discerning within the minutes when the moment takes place. All he knows is that he'll die trying to change the world before it changes him. Naisyn walks back over to him and lays her head on his shoulder.

"I love you, and I will never, *ever,* stop." She lifts her head up, places her hands on Jamar's face, and turns him to face her. "We'll get outta here, okay? And we'll figure things out, just like we always do."

Moisture builds in Jamar's eyes, which he desperately tries to stifle. He won't let these tears fall, not now.

"Nai, I'm sorry, but I'm not going wi—"

Three loud knocks interrupt Jamar's sentence. Naisyn swings around and leaps into the entrance of the balcony— her incisors instinctively extend into fangs and she hisses at their front door. When she looks back at Jamar, the glow of red and blue lights reflect off of his skin. He looks back at her with tears tumbling down his face.

"I love you."

And then he jumps.

INSIGHT: REFLECTION

All growth
is change,
but not all change
is growth.

– Augmented: Source

We all hope
that our actions, words,
and experiences can be
used to assist with
the progressive growth
of those closest to us,
but the reality is that our
knowledge can only
guide those who
truly seek guidance.

— Another Way: Jerome

I've heard people say
that running away
isn't the answer,
but that depends on
what answers one
has to choose from.

– Uneven 2

There's a very real,
and very fine line
between optimism
and negligence.

- The Undead Eye: Dr. Gren

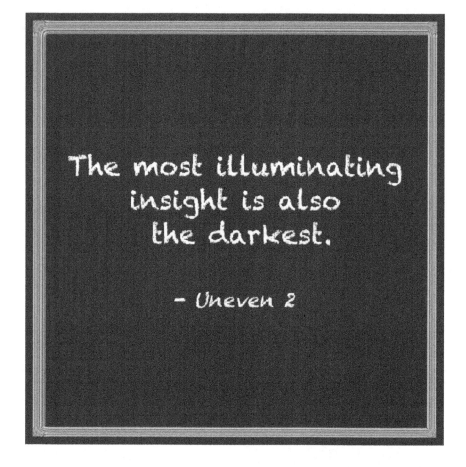

The most illuminating
insight is also
the darkest.

- Uneven 2

WESTJET

28NOV21 FLT/VOL 1565

WILTSHIRE/PETER MR
CABIN/CABINE: ECONOMY

DEP: SAN DIEGO
ARR: CALGARY INTL AB

DEP: 1:10PM
ARR: 5:30PM

BOARDING TIME /
HEURE D EMBARQUEMENT

ZONE
2

12:30PM

BOARDING PASS/ CARTE D EMBARQUEMENT
WILTSHIRE/PETER MR
28NOV21
FLT/VOL 1565

GATE /PRT
50

SEQ 012
PNR RKRAMJ

SEQ C12
PNR RKRAMJ

DEP: SAN
ARR: YYC

SEAT/PLACE
20D

SEAT/PLACE
20D

ELECTRONIC/ELECTRONIQUE
8382161993210/0

We're all born
with a barcode
into a world where
everything's for sale.

- Augmented: Inquiry

Words make you
believe things that
aren't real yet,
and maybe
never will be.

– The Undead Eye: Will

There's a time to listen,
and that time
should never
be wasted.

— Uneven 3

Normalcy is a line
drawn in the sand,
and each time
the tide rises
and washes it away,
it's never redrawn in
quite the same place
as it was before.

– The Undead Eye: Dr. Gren

Nothing that can
be experienced affects
one more than
the depth at which
the experience is felt.

– Broken Hands

A gold-paved
road to heaven
couldn't be offered
without the threat of
a soul-enslaving hell.

— Augmented: Inquiry

Making a martyr of
simplicity,
as demanded by
complexity,
is one of humanity's
more overrated and
unnecessary attributes.

– Uneven 3

How regrettable it is
when that which creates life
and beauty in the world
can be used to
create the exact opposite,
yet, how shortsighted
one must be to assume
that one creation
holds more value
than the other.

— Beware

Acceptance is the cure
for exclusion that
kills like venom
when overdosed.

- Augmented: Submersion

That's how the past
juggles with your sanity:
it makes the piranhas
look like puppies.

- Broken Hands

If the size of
one's reward is
dictated by the amount
they're willing to risk,
then gambling with
one's life should yield
the greatest return.

— Augmented: Inquiry

I've always felt like
life resembled an iceberg:
only a small portion was
visible on the surface
and that symbolized
life's aesthetic aspects,
but beneath the surface
held the majority of
what mattered—wisdom,
understanding, depth,
and clarity.

— Another Way: Lachelle

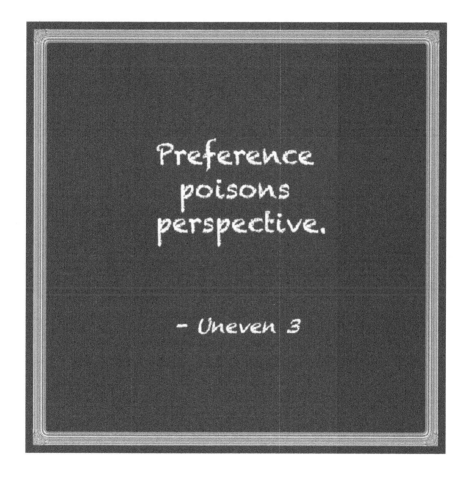

Maybe if you give people
a chance to be better,
they'll show you that
there's no such thing.

- The Undead Eye: Kennedy

Those without power
or purpose in their
own lives are the first
to seek power
and dominion over
the lives of others.

— Beware

AUGMENTED: SOURCE

O nce inter-dimensional travel was developed, along with a reproducible process to manipulate it, I'm not sure what people thought humanity would do with that caliber of technology, or how it would be beneficial. As a species, we're honestly too smart for our own preservation. Unlike every other life form on Earth, we were always going to be the ones to manifest our own extinction—the flood and ice age couldn't get rid of us, so we'd show the planet how it's done. It'd simultaneously be our one, unmatched, crowning achievement, as well as our last irreversible error—but I digress. Regarding the creation of the COAAD Station (Creator of Augmented Alternative Dimensions) used to reveal the IdT portals (inter-dimensional travel), I don't want to come across as the prototypical false prophet or fake oracle. I'm not the type to say they knew things would get crazy only *after* the insane asylum is filled to capacity, but in my opinion I'm one of the *few* people who legitimately saw this coming, and I definitely shouldn't have been.

As always, all of the signs of a lit match with the potential to rapidly become an uncontrolled forest fire were, like co-founders, there from the very beginning. There's only so far science can be pushed in the unblemished name of "progress", before it falls off the edge, bringing down everyone and everything within its proximity. Too often when an idea, procedure, or invention is considered to be brilliant or revolutionary, the first thing that's forgotten is that all growth is change, but not all change is growth. Even a monumental scientific advancement could be the first step towards an unmeasurably destructive direction. Do I feel that way because I was also there from the beginning? Although *I* wasn't plotting the project's course—that was all Dr. Leon— could I have just as easily been one of those warning signs? My contributions, however minimal they may have been, would've still acted as the addition of tinder to an already healthy flame, or, maybe I'm giving myself too much credit. In any case, it doesn't hold much significance anymore; what's done is done, all there is to do now is see what will be done next.

In retrospect, our environment suffered tremendously from an abundance of ego, and a deficit of accountability. We knew what we had in front of us, and the investors knew as well, but to the point of intoxication, we were at once too deeply mesmerized by, and impressed with, what we had managed to bring into being. Once one IdT portal was successfully opened, explored, and closed, what else could we have done other than try to summon specific dimensions to see how events could've played out differently? Unexpectedly, that wasn't what we were experiencing at all: the unit was producing the results we *asked for*, and initially, at varying levels of precision. For example, I may set these parameters for myself: "Hakeem Trenton, beloved billionaire astronaut, married to a loving supermodel-philanthropist with genius-level intellect"—hypothetically, of course—but what could be produced was a dimension where I'd caught an infection on a space mission that crippled me, and my wife creates a successful non-profit organization for disease research benefitting astronauts and others suffering currently incurable illnesses. The foundation then generates billions of dollars, of which, I'm awarded half of in our divorce settlement—not exactly what I would've been looking for. What I could do then is return from that nightmare, reword and rearrange the same parameters, and the dimension would recalibrate based on the alterations. COAAD humbly began as COAD, "Curator of Alternative Dimensions", but the extra A for Augmented, and the title of *Creator* was obviously warranted once its potential was realized. The moment it was confirmed that the device wouldn't just give us glimpses into existing parallel dimensions—for the initial purpose of researching potential technological advancements, and progressive geo-political initiatives—but allow variables to be entered that would, in part, *dictate* the global condition of the dimensions being displayed, we should've stopped. We should've, but we didn't, and we knew maybe a fraction of what we were doing. These weren't the fabled parallel dimensions we were dealing with, this was something else. On the other side of IdT there wasn't another Hakeem Trenton walking around, I would be the only me, just like I am here—we had traversed beyond science fiction. We didn't have the hand of God, but we did have three fingers; three parameters that we could enter into the unit in order to "drive" the COAAD to creation, before the portal became too unstable and crashed. COAAD was, in this way, like any other machine: it had its input and output limits that had to be respected for it to maintain the proper level of functionality. The power required to hold the door open to an augmented dimension could only be sustained for so long before the unit maxed out. Once the ceiling was met, it couldn't produce the additional energy necessary to sustain the connection any longer. Nevertheless, it didn't take long for the staff to informally replace the C in COAAD, for Creator, with a G, for God. *GOAAD* is what we called it almost exclusively after the first string of successful tests, and coincidentally, that ended up being the name that resonated with people the most.

I say "successful tests" fairly loosely, because once we knew what was possible as far as the portal's configuration, we just had to learn what the rules of the game were, which unfortunately, caused us to incur some losses. For much of the beta-tests we were able to avoid any casualties. Authenticating the 16 hour time-limit of portal stability, the precise wording and nine word arrangement required in order to prevent COAAD from randomizing the entered parameters, and the fact that after a2 ("attempt 2"; one's second consecutive IdT insertion) COAAD could only recreate the dimension from a2, but couldn't recreate a1, were all handled without measurable damage to participating personnel. Where issues arose was during a3. There was no way for us to forecast that returning one to their Birth Dimension from a third insertion couldn't be executed, and to find out definitively, we had to do what all have to do: we risked losing what was near to us, to gain that which could take us further. As a scientist and researcher, I've noticed the general assumption that those in my field must think like robots, when in reality, the calculations I rely on are the same as everyone relies on, the only difference is that I have to show my math. As *The Base Barter Principle* states: between two interacting entities there's always a level of physical or mental exchange; one's goods for another's services. Although it may go undetected by one, or both parties, and that which is exchanged may not be directly proportional, it exists and transpires nevertheless. Even those who give *freely* expect to trade their generosity for gratitude. Real lives were fed to the monster called Science; and from the monster we feed, grows a monster that feeds upon us.

It didn't take long for GOAAD to mutate into a god worthy of both praise and worship, and the Moses who led the exodus from the illusionary confines of our Egypt was none other than the lead designer, Dr. Izhar Ahad Leon. By this time, any of us could be Inserters—one who physically enters the data into the unit—and could deliver the requested dimension (to the "Requestor") on a1 with an average accuracy of 93% and easily achieve 100% accuracy on a2. Naturally, Dr. Leon still wanted to know more about the environment generated on a3. Before designing the blueprints for GOAAD—once he introduced the theoretical algorithm for IdT—he was already considered to arguably be the greatest scientific mind of the last two generations, and he didn't earn that designation by allowing his mind to be satiated by his successes. We were unable to return 13 participants from a3. The simulated test environment could only tell us so much, so we had to send them into live dimensions in order to properly test our hypotheses. Essentially all we learned from the trials was that no combination of the knowledge at our disposal was good enough to bring them back, and that wasn't good enough for Leon. The theory he proposed was that the increase in instability GOAAD displayed with each additional attempt was due to an increase in malleable energy. The increase *would* explain why on a2 our accuracy would jump to 100%: the more malleable the energy, the easier it was for the dimension to be molded by the inserted parameters (a1 then being necessary to generate the malleable energy needed for a successful a2 placement). The problem was that by a3, the energy was too malleable and couldn't be directed back to its origin i.e. back to the GOAAD station. What he was sincerely interested in was what the increased malleability did for the parameters we entered, and his hypothesis was that the percentage would rise beyond 100%; that if I was a billionaire astronaut on a2, I'd be a trillionaire by a3. The problem was that we hadn't been able to get anything back from a3, and that included communication of any variety. So Leon did what he did best: he got to work, and told us to do the same.

Eight months into the research, the entire team was exhausted, but Leon was sure we were getting closer. Out of the twelve of us left, maybe half actually still cared anymore. a1 and a2 worked perfectly well enough to prove that IdT could be safely manipulated and managed, and it was becoming clear this was the paranoid obsession of a mad scientist in mid-transformation. Jake Riser was the most vocal of us—as vocal as he could be anyway, without Leon kicking him out the door—so from what I was able to gather, it was his idea for the "suicide pact", as it were: we'd all get out through GOAAD—simple. It was either that, or remain working on a3 until our exclusive contracts ended, and the contracts didn't expire until the project was marked as closed. Leon was known to only accept working on projects that he fully controlled, so the project would be marked closed when he said it was and not a second sooner. Any of us in breach of contract wouldn't be able to work anywhere until he said so, and as one could imagine, that could take awhile. Jake could be pretty convincing when he wanted to be and, with these conditions, I was the only idiot who had reservations.

"So, you really wanna stay here and be his slave?!"

"Jesus, it's not just about *him*. Everyone's ready to just leave their families and their whole lives, and never look back? Just like that?!"

"Trenton, do you hear yourself, right now? You're right, it's not about him. We'll be walking out of one *pretty good* life, and walking into another one that we've designed *ourselves! We* built this, why shouldn't *we* benefit from it?"

"And what about the last Inserter? They'll have no one to send them to a2."

"Well, yeah—look, is it perfect? Obviously not. We're gonna randomize it; whoever ends up last, ends up last. They can either sit it out, or roll the dice on a1—you in? I mean, unless you've got a better idea." I didn't have a better idea, and I wasn't in, but it wouldn't kill me to help them. I volunteered to go last. Maybe I just didn't hate my life enough, or hate the job enough to permanently walk away from it all into some new reality that I patched together myself like Frankenstein's Monster. I didn't like my odds on a1 anyway; execution's an art form, and luck is for leprechauns, and I don't have a drop of Irish blood in my entire body.

After I sent the last of us through to a2, that's when I knew this had gotten out of control. Some of them left notes, others left nothing and hoped all the suspicion of their disappearance would fall on Leon, but they all apathetically walked away from every person that ever cared about them like it was nothing. How was that any different than the life they had now? How much *more* in control did they really think they were going to be in an alternative dimension that has all of the same rules as this one? Even with 100% accuracy no one knew how the dimension would develop longterm, and they wouldn't even have their 16 hours of test time. We're hardly talking about a precise blueprint when it's based on only three parameters, and these were people of *science* that were so blindly enchanted by the idea— something had to be done about it.

The team meeting we usually had to end each day looked more like a dinner date, but oddly, Leon didn't look terribly shocked either. He walked into the small conference room— already about ten minutes late—dropped a folder at the head of the table, hung his white coat over his seat, and looked around the room indifferently.

"Where's everyone else?"

Before I arrived, I considered making up some elaborate story, but it'd already been a long day, and I wasn't in the mood. In this case, I don't think I could've concocted a scenario more outlandish than the one that actually took place.

"They're not coming."

"Is that so?" He unbuttons his sleeves and begins rolling them up his forearms.

"Unfortunately, yes."

"And, why would that be?" Did *I* get sent to an alternative dimension also? Because there's no way this conversation is happening like this; then again, I'm sure the gears will shift soon enough.

"The team, minus myself, is all gone. They decided to—"

"Take GOAAD…to a2, I assume—am I right?" There's no way he could know that, this place is a vault. Not one camera, or cell phone, or anything that can record an image of any kind in any way; just what amounts to a full cavity search on arrival and departure.

"You already knew?"

"Lucky guess. Glad you were smarter than they were, or, was it just some bad luck that you had to be the one left with the check?"

"Yeah, something like that."

"Not a problem, I only needed one witness anyway. I cracked it." He picks up the folder he has on the table and waves it side-to-side in front of his face.

"a3?!"

"Of course a3." I, like everyone else who was working here, put up with Leon because he is, in fact, a genius, but I never thought after eight months he'd stroll into one of these pointless meetings with an answer for this thing. "Since it's just you and me left anyway, I'll dazzle you with the math when I get back. Let's go, Inserter." He can't be thinking of testing this.

"You're not serious, are you?"

"What? What else would I be *other* than serious? Do you think I'd be joking? Because that'd be a really weird thing to joke about."

"No, of course, I just meant—"

"I know what you meant, Trenton. Do you know *why* I have a Pulitzer? That's rhetorical, obviously—it's because I mark my projects closed once every question *asked* has been answered, and every question *unasked* has been proven irrelevant, and not a goddamn second sooner. I'm doing what everyone else is too lazy to do, because I know one thing: you can't discover anything new under the sun, if you're afraid to stare into it." He picks up his jacket, folds it in half lengthwise, and tosses it over his shoulder. "C'mon, let's go."

We called the space where the GOAAD was located The Throne Room, and the hallway that led up to it The Green Mile, and I was walking in alone, with the king himself, because we were the last ones left—it was a cubism painting come to life: nothing was the shape that it used to be. Leon scanned his badge and pulled the door to The Throne Room all the way open—that way he wouldn't have to hold it for me—and walked in as I followed. He threw his jacket onto the three-seater couch to his right and placed his folder on the side table nearest to it. He headed straight for GOAAD without saying a word, so I made my way over to the Insertion Console. Just as I sat down, I heard him say, "You'll need the folder. The parameters are in there." Of course they are, he could've easily *told them* to me, but I guess that would've been too boring. I'd like to be pissed off that he thinks right now is the time to be a diva, but I guess I'd have an attitude also if all my friends used my favorite toy to abandon me. Once I got the folder and brought it back with me to the console, I noticed the weight of it was significant— maybe the formulas were as "dazzling" as he was boasting. I found the parameters and powered-up GOAAD, and when I checked to see if Leon was in place he was already laying down flat inside of the unit giving me a thumbs up. He was ready, I was ready, I got IdT engaged, and in exactly 18 seconds he was gone. I bring him back, send him, and when I bring him back the second time, we prepare to, hopefully, step into the unknown, and back once more. This time he signals me to wait, sits up, opens the hatch door, and pokes his head out.

"Start audio calibration at 8dB."

"We never start at 8dB."

"Right. This is why I'm specifically *telling you* to start at 8dB." This is honestly the most Leon and I have conversed one-on-one, and now I almost wish that I left with the others. "If by some miracle a3 is a disaster, I want to make sure you hear everything that's happening *as* it's happening. And when it's greater than anything imagined, I want that coming through flawlessly."

"8dB—set." He opened his mouth to say something but then didn't—was that hesitation? Can genius' even do that? The hatch door closes, he reassumes the position laying down, and gives me a thumbs up once again. I must be projecting; hesitation couldn't survive in that thing.

"Good luck, asshole." I engage IdT, and he's gone.

Nothing to do now but wait, so I get the chair adjusted to recline but end up bumping the bottom of the desk when I lean back, causing a few pages to fall out of Leon's folder. "Damnit!" I gather the loose pages together and take a look at what he came up with, and there's nothing good there, nothing even close to good. He figured out how to counteract an increase in the environments malleability in order to transmit sound, but that's it. There's also a handwritten note stuck in there also, and it's addressing *me*:

"Hakeem, this isn't my Birth Dimension, this is my a2. I thought maybe from here I could figure out a3, but mathematically nothing's any clearer. This folder has everything I've found. More than what's on the server. I don't know what will happen when I'm gone, so you might need this. If I'm correct, the numbers point to an influx in foreign DNA signatures all on a3. The malleability is from the dimension HOLDING people, and I don't know what—"

Without warning audio blares through the speakers like a stadium full of airhorns. I lunge at the volume—knocking Leon's entire folder to the floor in the process—and turn it down to 0dB, yet whatever's going on in there is still ear-shatteringly fierce! The sound isn't a glitch either, it's coming from wherever a3 led Leon and it's reading directly from GOAAD. It's so loud there's no individual discernible sounds, so it could be anything: a natural disaster, a group of animals dying, a war zone, a slaughterhouse, or the daily news. What the hell do I do with this?! All of the equipment I've used is hardwired together, and trying to problem solve when your ears feel like they could be bleeding turns out to be mildly distracting. *BOOM, BOOM, BOOM!* I should've known security would come knocking soon. They're motioning for me to turn it down, and I'm shrugging to let them know that I can't do anything, and that they need to get in here. One of them finally understands and scans in.

"What the hell's going on?!"

"No clue! I turned it all the way down!"

"You can't shut this thing off?!" He starts to walk towards GOAAD, and I cut his path off.

"No! *Absolutely* not! Everything would overload! Can't you kill the speakers?!" He turns to the other three guys he brought with him.

"Can we just kill the sound?! This guy says he can't—"

POP! POP! The speakers submit to the unyielding pressure, and the room is rescued by the valiance of silence. Everyone's rubbing their ears, I imagine because their ringing with the same heart monitor, flat-line tone that mine are. On one of the monitors I can still see the visual reading of the sound coming through. Whatever's going on in that dimension is still getting transmitted, and it's not dissipating at all—what kind of hell did Leon fall into? Nothing with GOAAD or the console seems effected, and now that it's finally quiet, I can figure out what Leon wanted me to do with this folder. When I turn to tell security that I can handle things from here, two of them are standing beside each other shuffling through papers. They picked up Leon's notes and the folder that I knocked to the floor—this might not be good.

"What are these? Craig told us there shouldn't be any paper copies of anything anywhere. 'Absolutely everything should be digital and on the server'—that's what he told me."

"Right—yes, and that is correct—these were just some last minute instructions from Dr. Leon. Nothing that won't be uploaded." I tried smiling casually and acting nonchalant, but I didn't study theoretical astrophysics because I felt like my acting prowess was too far ahead of its time. The security guard who seems to be the leader looks at the papers he's holding, then over at the papers the guard to his left is holding.

"That's not what this note says. The note says this is 'more than what's on the server.' See?" He holds up Leon's note so I can see it, and smirks at me smugly. "I think I'll get this to Craig."

"I need that folder and the notes to finish my work, okay? Do *whatever* you want with them when I'm done."

"I think I'll get this to Craig. *You* can talk to him about it."
He turns to his minions, "Alright, let's go."

Thomas Craig is just Macrokite's brainless CEO, but he's
not dumb enough *not* to destroy everything his considerably
dumber security guards are about to present him with. I
know what I have to do, I just have to figure out a way to do
it, but first, a3. Leon's gone, but by what I was able to read
from his note, he saw that coming anyway. I import the a3
file into a digital audio workstation, and finally adjust it
enough that it's at a level where my ears won't explode on
impact. I plug headphones into the console, and hope there's
something useful. There's still a layer of distortion in the file
that the program couldn't fully remove, but it's easily 80%
clearer now, and what I hear is nauseating: the recording
contained the voices of people—*a lot* of people—and they
were screaming as if their limbs were being slowly torn from
their bodies. It was horrifying. Barely audible through the
brutality was another voice, still yelling, but in a different
way, almost like—was someone saying my name? It had to be
Leon, right? Who or what else could it be? The audio
transmitter sent the signal, so he at least must've survived
where he was long enough to turn it on. Over the tormented
screams it was still difficult to hear him, but I wrote down
everything I could understand.

"HAAAKEEEM!…IT DOWN!…SHUT…PEOPLE…KNOW
NOW! RIGHT NOW!…GET…AND…THE…CRAIG WON'T!…
FILES…THE…ASAP!…91…6…8…03…3…THAT?!…46…7…
90…834!…IT!…HELL! HELL!"

He started screaming like everyone else, reminiscent of
nothing I've ever heard before, nor heard since, and then it
went dead. It wasn't a whole lot to go on, but I'm assuming

the fragmented number I heard was important. I knew I had to get a copy of the files off of the server before Craig had someone from Macrokite tamper with them, and blow the whistle on this whole project. I couldn't take these people down by myself.

I should've just went into IdT like the others, or at the very least, minded my business and nothing more. I accessed the server. I glued together the splintered pieces of the pin number Leon was yelling to me from a3, and I did it: I managed to export a copy of the COAAD files and waltz away from the facility with them in a nervous sweat...only to discover everything was redacted. Not *everything*, but they definitely made sure it wouldn't be easy reading. I filled in the blanks where I could, and I took the information public, but things didn't proceed as I'd hoped.

I expected the backlash, the death threats, having to be put under police protection—my car was stolen—I knew things wouldn't be easy for me, what I didn't know is how the general public would react. From what I gathered via social media, and traditional media sources, is that it was basically 65/35 in favor of those who were actually mad that COAAD was never created and maneuvered into a version of mass production available for public consumption. I'd explained in numerous interviews how detrimental COAAD would've been, how easy it was for people to abandon the lives they knew for the augmented dimensions, like a hermit crab discarding a shell that no longer fit its purposes. Macrokite's plotted trajectory was to have these things in every research facility, and on every college campus that had a budget for one. I played the last audio file Leon transmitted, and I saw more reactions to it being a hoax than a legitimate reason for caution and concern. Those who were labeled as, or labeled themselves as, "believers" called wherever Leon sent the recording from "Antithinai", but I called it what he called it: Hell. Throughout the ordeal I was forced to recognize the depths at which I neither understood society, nor the people that it was comprised of. I couldn't tell if *I* was crazy or if they were, or if sanity and insanity existed at all. I wanted to know if what I did was right or wrong, and the answer arrived before I knew it, like a defibrillator to the chest.

Two years after all whistles had been blown, when the name Macrokite was most notably used as a near science fiction pop-culture reference, and my name was usually mispronounced or forgotten entirely, the aftermath of my heroic deeds appeared on my favorite investigative journalism docu-series, *The Iris*. Episode one of the three-part investigation was on a reported new technological black market: people had resurrected the COAAD plans, and were building their own terribly reproduced models of the unit based on the redacted design documents. If someone was smart enough to build the machine, then they should know that was the easy part, but if those files were allowed to get out, and people thought they had everything they needed, they would soon find out they were missing a critical amount of information—assuming they cared. They wouldn't know how to prevent randomizing the parameters in order to control where people ended up, so they'd have to test the units out just like we did, and people wouldn't make it back.

Most of what wasn't redacted was marketing material that robotically sang COAADs praises—how flawless it was, and how we were "walking into a limitless future" blah, blah, blah. It was almost like…like Macrokite knew the files would get out eventually, and when they did, they'd still be the mythic name behind the greatest piece of technology that was too revolutionary to be kept alive. This was my fault. I'm the one that let this monster out. I set this all in motion, and now it was *way* further than my arms could reach.

The title of episode was Code Name *GOAAD: The God With Heaven For Sale.*

AUGMENTED: INQUIRY

Everyone who needed to know about GOAAD[11] knew about GOAAD—that's how I was told it worked, anyway. I knew about it, but I didn't think I needed to know about it, so I wasn't really sure how to feel about that. Apparently, it was for one of three kinds of people: those who had everything they wanted, but none of what they needed; those who had everything they needed, but none of what they wanted; and those who had neither. I'd seen what happened to people when everything they wanted was finally theirs, and I'd only wish that on my worst enemy. What I wanted could kill me, and what I needed would save me. Honestly, all I wanted was what I needed, like cacti in the desert storing water between the infrequent, but timely rainfalls. Although I believed that thought when I was thinking it, I simultaneously knew that I could be over-rationalizing my situation in order to appreciate it more— what else could I do? Either I forced myself to fall in love with what I had, knowing if I had the choice I'd replace all of it, or, I lived in a perpetual state of resentment, incubating a deep depression, leading to either a slow suicide over time, or one that took me instantly. Other than that decision, I didn't grapple much with the luxury of indecisiveness because I didn't have many options at my disposal. After I

---

[11] *God of Augmented Alternative Dimensions;* the device used to send Requestors into alternative dimensions.

was laid off and evicted from my apartment, I did what was necessary to make a life for myself—to survive. Luckily for me, we're all born with a barcode.

It was never my plan to settle, to deify the lesser of two evils, worship it as my savior, and live ensnared in a religion of my own creation[12]. I never planned to preach sermon after sermon to myself about how my life was okay because it wasn't as bad as it could be, or as bad as others who were worse off. Yet, that's where I was in my life when I heard about GOAAD—a god promising a prize other than the Earth for the meek to inherit.

The rumors were all equally insane. People would go into the machine as burger flippers, working every miserable hour they could get, but then appear in a new dimension as a trust-fund baby with more money than they could spend in a lifetime; from an unknown starving artist, to an internationally-recognized celebrity—anything anyone could think of. Well, almost anything. It's supposed to keep your DNA intact, so, sadly, I couldn't go in human and have them create a dimension where I was a jellyfish drifting through

---

[12] Displeasing Decision Consolation: When having to choose between two undesirable options, this is the process of making oneself more at ease with the decision by creating, or manipulating, aspects of the selected choice into a more favorable light—albeit a false one. This allows one to produce a convincing scenario where they have an appreciation of something they never wanted to begin with, therefore decreasing the possibility of increasing dissatisfaction and disappointment regarding their selection. In other words, if one can either invent or imagine a set of desired characteristics about a selection they never wanted, they can fool themselves into liking, or even loving, something they previously never cared for.

the pristine blue waters of the open ocean. Either way, it'd be a brand new life that I could customize the way that I wanted; to be planted in the midst of prosperity and freedom so that I could grow myself, and my environment, to my liking; to be given a real chance not to make the same mistakes I'd already made.

The other crazy part was that people were saying that the GOAAD *Inserters* (those who program and send people into these alternative dimensions) weren't all created equal, that some of them were better than others—knew things that the others didn't. I could tell them what I want, but if they didn't enter it into GOAAD correctly, I could end up being a celebrity's maid instead of a celebrity chef. You get what you pay for, and the more you have to spend, the higher the skill level you can afford. Nevertheless, like all proper gods, a gold-paved road to heaven couldn't be offered without the threat of a soul-enslaving hell, and nothing I've ever heard of sounded worse than *Antithinai*. Out of all the rumors, this one especially had to be discussed at night, around a campfire, with a cheap flashlight pointed up at your nose—it was the ultimate ghost story. Antithinai was nicknamed the "cell of screams and silence", and it was rumored to be a solitary confinement cell where you're surrounded by people also stuck in cells suffering. None of you can help each other, you just keep yelling, and screaming for help, and trying to break through the door until you've beaten your body to a paste, one limb at a time, until you're dead. It was the quintessential reminder that GOAAD was, and would remain, a gamble for as long as people kept making them—if the stories were to be taken literally, of course. The problem was that no one could dispel the rumor since no one returns or can communicate from their third IdT (inter-dimensional travel) attempt (a3). The only one who figured out how to communicate from a3 was the guy who invented GOAAD, and all that's known about Antithinai was based on the leaked Trenton Files—which supposedly came from that same inventor. Combine that with the imaginations of whoever had time to add more sprinkles to the ice cream, and what's served is a bowl of mostly unanswered questions.

It's been said that Heaven and Hell are rooms on the same floor. Apparently, a1 was hardly ever what people asked for, a2 was usually closer to what they asked for, so in theory, a3 must be exactly what they asked for or even better—as long as the Inserter can keep from sending you to a cell which may, or may not exist. Then again, no one knew if that was absolutely the case either. If the size of one's reward is dictated by the amount they're willing to risk, then gambling with one's life should yield the greatest return. Regrettably for many of us that isn't true, instead we end up becoming fallen soldiers: risking it all in exchange for becoming a memory.

Inserters were constantly moving the GOAAD stations so that they weren't found by the police. If they were found, and the Inserter would say that someone was already in IdT, the officer used to have to wait for them to pull that person out. But now, after multiple instances of Inserters lying and using the opportunity to get away, if there's a raid they just shut it all down without question. If someone *is* actually in there and the machine is shut off improperly, no one knows for sure what happens to them—maybe they die, maybe they don't. Each GOAAD is built with varying levels of sophistication, and Inserters can charge more for that too, so most of them do. For example, some have more detailed life monitoring systems than others to keep track of the

Requestors (those paying Inserters for IdT), clearer communication modules, or have had more attention given to the build quality. Naturally, the cheaper GOAADs and Inserters quickly get reputations for their units or operators failing in one way or another. Things like sloppy a1 and a2 placements, shaky communication systems, etc., which is why it's best to bring at least one other person with you. I've done my research.

I suppose what would actually be *best* is if we all just fixed our own lives in the dimension we were born in, but we're human, we make things to make existing easier. We find a scenic route and then we create a shortcut. We're all authors without editors, writing out the story of our lives in permanent marker on a bathroom stall wall, hoping to get it right without having to cross anything out. Hoping that, even if it's never seen by anyone other than us, for once, we said exactly what we wanted to say, exactly how we wanted to say it. Too bad it doesn't always work out.

There's a lot in my life that I've had to put a line through, that I've marked over so many times all that can be seen is a black spot on the page. I have too many memories that I wish I couldn't remember, decisions I wish I didn't have to make, and exchanges where I gave more than I received to get what little I needed. Once I reviewed the writings of my life, it was clear GOAAD had found one of its own. I renounced my religion, crafted of false idols, and accepted GOAAD—the

God of Augmented Alternative Dimensions—alone as the One, and the True.

However, IdT isn't cheap. For those who don't have much, the usual path to get there is by planning to save for a lifetime, or selling everything they have that carries value. I chose the latter, because I didn't have a lifetime to wait for heaven. I would say that I wasn't proud of the way I earned the money necessary to start over, but by whose standards should I use as the measurement? One created and perpetrated by imperfect, upright walking animals that are incapable of escaping contradiction? Who exactly is the creator of where my pride should rightfully reside? I see no one but myself. Although my ticket into heaven cost me the life of one who had no say in their own, we're all born with a barcode into a world where everything's for sale, and *her* price tag had more zeroes at the end than mine did. When I tell God's angels what my heaven should look like, I'll make sure that my daughter is there as well, and that she has a mother who gives her more the second time around.

AUGMENTED: SUBMERSION

When I arrived on the other side of my second IdT[13] attempt, what I noticed initially was the regrettable similarity it had to my life in my Birth Dimension. Everyone who knew me thought they knew who I was—everyone except for me. I recognized my face, eyes, and body when I looked in the mirror, but other than that, the learning curve was alpine and tedious. I'd been born directly into adulthood as the parent of this life that I had to learn, raise, and exercise vigilance over, so it was a lot to get accustomed to. That was nine years ago.

When I left, I remember the over-generalized understanding being that people jumped into a GOAAD[14] because they were suicidal, but I never contemplated killing myself, or hiring someone to do it, for even a moment. I love being alive and I love living life, I just hated the version of life I was born into. Convinced there was a massive rain

---

[13] Inter-dimensional Travel

[14] *God of Augmented Alternative Dimensions;* the device used to send Requestors into alternative dimensions.

cloud constantly above me and just ahead of me, I thought I was one of the unlucky, animated corpses who had been cursed by an unseen hand to roam the Earth miserably. Was I to be the ever-stalked victim of this looming, omniscient mass that hovered above me? I felt cursed by the rain, but I now know that the rain was existence powering that which existed. The rain is what hydrates life—it keeps life alive—without it, life would suffocate in a passionately barren drought that only grew drier until it turned to ash, as if the more brittle it became, the stronger its satisfaction. I didn't know that the slow traverse through the rain was the journey of life itself; it wasn't the curse, but the blessing—the curse was created by resistance. When one calmly makes their way through the rain, the rain is experienced as feeling light and falls upon them softly. When one moves faster in an attempt to escape the rain, the harder the same rain seems to hit them, and the heavier it appears to be—resistance creates resistance. A calm environment can feel like an aggressive one if, I myself, am aggressive. The gentle shower takes on the properties of a rainstorm because I've allowed myself to become as agitated as the lightning and thunder. What I was running from was preventing me from dying; what I was running from is what I should've been walking with. It wasn't that my life was difficult, I was. At the time I didn't understand, and I couldn't see how these aspects connected to each other. Life wasn't affecting me, *I* was affecting *it,* and there was no augmented dimension where that still wouldn't be the breath rising and falling within the lungs of my environment.

My heaven is one where, upon my arrival, I was the standard that all aspired to attain or surpass—naturally, to embody perfection, I envisioned a life that was the polar opposite of my own. I vacated a space where the leaders of the entire world were either living to lead others to follow, or followers in disguise themselves. I saw that I had ascended far beyond their embellished height, and that the example I would set, when I was in a position to lead, would be one that led followers to leadership of oneself. This new home dimension was supposed to have granted me a life where I could fulfill my potential, and evidently it did that, along with much more.

We're all alive to reconnect with ourselves, all alive to be who we are, but not everyone sees that. In my Birth Dimension, who I was only earned me the privilege of being constantly berated and force-fed the overcooked scraps of my failures—another advantage I misread as being an affliction. Here, in circadian rhythm, each of my days are symbolic portrayals of every bleak, Renaissance Era oil-painting inspired by the Passion of Christ. *I'm* now the standard that's impossible to satisfy, as well as the appointed ruler of many, until my death. With each day I'm alive I grow more detested by those I govern in both depth and width, as if impaled by an iceberg. In the humble eyes of my audience, I typified everything they never knew they wanted, then reminded them how they would never be able to obtain it. I'm living in the blood-scorching, dark side, of the lethal injection that is said to be the remedy for those on the outside looking in: acceptance. Acceptance is the cure for exclusion that kills like venom when overdosed. As royalty, I was lifted up so high, loved and accepted so deeply, that soon the same characteristics which first inspired admiration began brewing animosity like a distillery. I'd unintentionally set the bar so high that those looking up at me thought it easier to chop the bar down, than fail reaching the thin air of it's disorienting height.

I boiled in the sun and cried tears of blood and regret for a year straight. The only difference now is that my tears are dust in the wind where the immortal drips of the Great Nile proved an unworthy adversary against the test of time. I thought time would then be on my side. I thought it would change me and mold me into a naturally occurring, irrationally occurring monument rising directly from the fabric of this manicured dimension, but never did. Time taught me that time doesn't change us, it unfolds us, like the recipient of a handwritten letter. Each section that's turned to face the reader only reveals more and more of what lay inside all along. That's what time did to me, it turned to the page I had hidden inside where all of the dark spells and forbidden secret potions were scribbled in rushed shorthand. Time pressed the sorcery of my ego into my face so I could see what brought me here. I was now living in this place where the churning, internal lava pit of my arrogance erupted into the faces of whom I'd enraged: I wanted to be recognized as the standard because I knew I was better than everyone else. Seeing as I was ritually offered up to the demons of inferiority, I survived by slaughtering demons who screamed til their death—lungs flooded with blood—before severing and hanging their heads as examples of my conquests. Unwisely, I dispatched my demons without first understanding them, so I was bound to become a demon myself—*this* is the great lesson. If one is inspired by dark intentions to find the light, the light will blind them before it guides them. Nine years after first setting foot into heaven, my sight has yet to return.

ABOUT THE AUTHOR

Sean Aeon lives to create. Every conversation is inspiring; every observation is a story. He writes to breathe life into fleeting thoughts hoping that they will give birth to ideas, ignite intrigue, and spark dialogue. Maybe your head is overflowing with ideas that you don't know what to do with. Maybe you think you need a degree, or need people with notable social or professional status to tell you that your ideas are good enough to be heard. You don't need any of that. Just get it all out. Don't just talk about it, don't just think about it—write, now.

Made in the USA
Monee, IL
26 July 2021